THE ROOM WAS SUDDENLY SILENT

"I don't think you're the Gunsmith at all, mister! I think you're a fake."

"That's right," said Clint. "I'm not the Gunsmith. My name is Clint Adams."

"Mister, you're full of it."

"Jesse, don't . . ." one of his companions said.

But he was too late—the cowboy's hand struck like a snake to his six-gun while Clint Adams still held his beer in his gunhand. Within the next second—or even less, Jesse cleared his gun from its holster. The Gunsmith dropped his glass of beer. Before it hit the floor, Clint Adams had his Colt out and up, and a single shot sent Jesse's gun flying across the barroom, while a scream of pain, rage, and astonishment was torn from the cowboy's mouth . . .

Also in THE GUNSMITH series

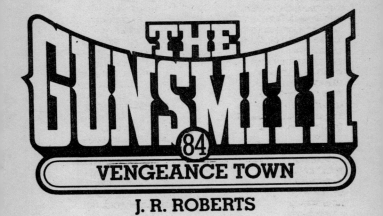

THE GUNSMITH

84

VENGEANCE TOWN

J. R. ROBERTS

JOVE BOOKS, NEW YORK

THE GUNSMITH #84: VENGEANCE TOWN

A Jove Book/published by arrangement with
the author

PRINTING HISTORY
Jove edition/December 1988

ISBN: 0-515-09849-3

Jove Books are published by The Berkley Publishing Group,
200 Madison Avenue, New York, New York 10016.
The name "JOVE" and the "J" logo
are trademarks belonging to Jove Publications, Inc.

PRINTED IN THE UNITED STATES OF AMERICA

10 9 8 7 6 5 4 3 2 1

ONE

The Black Hills of Dakota were a long way behind Clint Adams and Duke, his big black gelding, as the burnished sun slipped behind the darkening clouds on the western horizon. The Gunsmith had been idling along in search of a marked trail. He was getting low in provisions. His four canteens—one for himself, one for Duke, and two for the bay team pulling his gunsmithing wagon—were each less than half full. He wasn't worried, but now as he drove the wagon around the southern base of a towering butte he decided he'd better start moving along at a quicker pace.

It wasn't long after he'd made this decision that he discovered a trail, and without any indication from him, the team's pace quickened, as though they'd known all along what they'd been looking for. Duke, halter-tied to the endgate, nickered in response as he picked up his gait.

The trail immediately led them up through a thick stand of spruce and pine and then opened onto a high ledge that held a sweeping view of the long, wide valley that rolled south and west toward Sunshine Wells.

Because he was higher up here, the sun was not as close to the horizon as it had been; suddenly the sky seemed brighter, the day longer. He was just thinking that they could get water down at the river when he heard the bark of muskets, and his eyes snaked to the trail below, which cut almost through the center of the plain.

Speeding westward was a stagecoach, its driver cursing his six-horse team as he cracked his long whip at them; while his partner, the guard, was firing futilely at a half-dozen war-whooping Indians in blazing pursuit.

The redmen were gaining quickly on the coach as they fanned out, making it harder for the guard to reach a target. The Gunsmith could see how they were painted up and obviously looking for trouble as they spread wider now, clearly bent on intercepting the stage,

Young bucks jumping their reservation, Clint Adams was thinking, as he unlimbered his Winchester; and it looked, too, as though they were loaded not only with ammunition but whiskey. Indeed, one was so drunk he fell off the back of his horse with a wild cry of surprise. But this didn't help the guard on the racing coach, Clint could see, for it was impossible for him to score with his shotgun at that range. The Gunsmith pulled to a stop, groundhitched his team, untied Duke, mounted him, and galloped down a shallow draw; away from the oncoming stage and its pursuers. He had decided on a stand of cottonwoods where he would wait for the coach to pass him. Then he would surprise the renegade bucks from the flank or rear.

Atop the bouncing, clattering, racing coach, the driver—one Casper Trout—had spotted the lone rider on the big black gelding and bellowed down to his passengers and to his guard behind him, who was having a tough time staying aboard, let alone drawing a bead on the galloping foe to their rear.

"We got more company yonder! Could be friendly. 'Ceptin' they're headin' away."

Two of the four passengers were slumped low in their seats, trying to protect themselves. The two others were overridden by their curiosity, and were foregoing safety, at least for the moment. These were a black-garbed woman and a skinny, feverish-looking man in town clothes; and they were glued to the windows of the bouncing coach.

The feverish man was inquisitive by nature, being a member of the fourth estate, and he was deciding that the woman in black, who had been so retiring and even silent until now, was somehow morbidly fascinated by the attacking redskins.

"You'll see them better from over this side, ma'am."

"More?" she asked, and the newspaperman caught the anxiety in her voice.

"I count six. And look! Somebody's shooting at them from those trees over there!" He let out a sudden bellow of surprise. "He is charging them! My God, one man! Excuse me, miss—ma'am. But look, on that big black horse!"

Indeed, the Gunsmith and Duke were throwing the liquored braves into confusion by doing the totally unexpected. They were charging; the Gunsmith gripped his reins in his teeth while he fired his Winchester rapidly at the attackers.

The Indians were too surprised, not to mention too inebriated, to respond with any effectiveness. The Gunsmith nicked one along his neck, knocked another one off his horse, and managed to masterfully create the confusion and sudden caution that he had hoped for. In another moment the six had turned their horses, picked up their fallen comrades, and were racing away.

Meanwhile, atop the swaying, dashing coach, the guard—Toby Tubbs by name—informed the driver Casper Trout that the engagement was ended.

"They're haulin' out. Looks like that rider there scared the shit outta them."

"Plus the rotgut, I'd reckon," put in Casper Trout. "Hell, we'd of out-run the buggers anyways."

The guard who had had his troubles with Trout's know-it-all manner, now found a welcome opening. " 'Less you ease off on them hosses, Casper, you're gonna founder the team. And the switch station's a good while off."

Casper Trout mumbled something inaudible, but Toby Tubbs smiled at having scored, evening the little battle that was never recognized overtly, but had been carried on for at least a couple of years.

"They gone; they quit for sure?" Casper asked, hardening his tone a good bit.

"They dropped back a good piece now, heading east, it looks like."

"Good enough. We'll rest 'em down by the ford there."

In the coach the skinny newspaperman man informed

his fellow passengers of the news; the battle was over, and the red devils had been routed by the lone rider on the black horse.

"We're safe enough now," he assured them, though speaking mostly to the woman in black, who had returned to her seat beside him. The other two travelers, both men, nodded with evident relief that the episode was ended.

Clint Adams had followed the stage down to the river ford, all the while keeping a strong eye on the area toward which the Indians had ridden.

When the coach finally stopped, the Gunsmith drew rein. He dismounted a short distance from the coach and nodded as the driver and guard thanked him.

"What's your next stop?" he asked, as he took out his field glasses.

"Just the switch station." Casper Trout spat out a stream of tobacco, getting some of it on the nearest horse's rump.

Clint had his field glasses trained on the flats but saw nothing unusual. He didn't expect the braves to return.

"We make Sunshine at sundown," Casper said. "Good town, Sunshine Wells. You know it, mister?"

"Can't say so," said Clint.

"Well, mister, you want to follow us in, your supper won't cost you a dime. Compliments of the Goocher Stage Line."

Then Toby Tubbs said, "Think them rascals has had enough?"

"They'll be sore-headed pretty soon, when the rotgut works its way down to their toes," the Gunsmith said. "In a little while they'll likely regroup and come back

for another try. By then we'll be well clear of here."
He returned the binoculars to his saddlebag, and was
about to comment severely on the nature of anyone who
would sell rattlesnake whiskey to reservation Sioux,
when he spotted a female face at the window of the
coach.

"I guess they sure enough were drunk," said Toby
Tubbs.

"That they were," agreed Clint Adams. "Else they
wouldn't have quit so easy."

But the face in the coach disappeared as Clint moved
closer to the driver and his team. Inside the coach the
thin, high-strung man suddenly chuckled, raised himself in his seat, and looked at the lady in black.

"You know what that there feller is?" he asked, his
pale face alight with special news.

"I must admit I don't," the lady said, speaking with
a well-modulated, eastern accent.

"Fact is, if that feller knew who I was he might even
be a mite hostile to me."

"Who are you?" she asked with a puzzled frown.
"Should I know?"

A sheepish grin stole over the other man's face.

"No special reason to know me. My name's Abner
Frolicher, and I am a member of the fourth estate, that
is to say, the press. My bottom dollar says that feller's
the Gunsmith."

"You mean you're a newspaperman?" she asked,
looking directly into his vague eyes.

"Uh—yes," he replied, shaken slightly by her forth-
right response.

"And you happen to know this man—Gun something-or-other?"

"He is known as the Gunsmith. Actually, his name is Clint Adams."

"I see."

Abner Frolicher was about to expand on his narrative and intended to ask the lady her name, but suddenly the man known as the Gunsmith appeared at the window of the stagecoach.

"You folks all right in here?"

The men nodded vigorously; but Clint Adams hardly noticed. His attention was riveted on the dark-haired beauty who was sitting beside the rusty-looking little man in the derby hat.

"I'm Clint Adams," he said, touching the brim of his Stetson with his forefinger.

"Pleased to meet you, sir," the lady in black replied. "And may I offer you our very deep thanks."

"If I can be of any assistance to you, Miss . . ."

"Thank you, you've done more than anyone might expect in the present emergency. I am most grateful." She seemed to remember the others then, and her eyes swept over the three men. "We all are, I am sure."

"I'll be riding in behind you," Clint said. "If there should be any need . . ."

He let the rest of it hang, turning away with the imprint of a pair of beautiful dark hazel eyes set in a very white face, and a bosom that was high, firm, and utterly desirable.

As he stepped into the stirrup of his worn stock saddle, his eyes ran over the trail ahead, then cut to their back trail. There was no sign of any human.

"I'm ready to skin this team here, mister," said Casper Trout, streaking tobacco juice between his wheel team to hit plumb center on the whiffletree. "Lemme hear the word."

"Let's move then." And Clint Adams glanced up quickly into the window of the stagecoach, but the woman who had somehow managed not to let him know her name was sitting well back in her seat and out of view.

TWO

"Somebody's got to handle her," the tall man with the droopy brown mustache was saying. "I think it ought to be Doc."

Doc Joyner looked at his two companions, a sour expression on his long, gray face. "Like I told you, Harry, and you, Felix, when you wanted me to write his widow, I aim to have nothing to do with it."

"But you're the town doctor; you're the one likely to soften it for her when she gets here," said Harry Bones.

"What do you want me to tell her? That her husband was shot to death while trying to escape from jail? That he'd been arrested for a brutal murder? I told you, dammit, when I signed the death certificate, I don't want any part of it. Harry, you're the lawman in this burg, and Felix, you're head of the town council—well, after Torb Mill, anyway. . . ." He was shaking his gray head, reaching to his pocket for his pipe and tobacco.

The three men were standing in Joyner's office on Main Street. A letter had come from the widow of the man named Todd Gandy who had been arrested and then shot to death during an escape attempt.

"She ought to be here today, maybe tomorrow the latest," said Felix Porterhouse, number-two man on the town council, who was wishing that the head man, Torb Mill, was there instead of himself. But Torb—typically—had scoffed at the notion of greeting the condemned man's widow and had told Felix that if he and Joyner and Harry Bones felt the need to socialize with the widow of a murderer—and not just any murderer, but Ephraim Crosby's killer—then they could do it on their own. He was shut of the affair. The killer was rightfully dead and buried, without a single wet eye in town.

"I know she'll come right away," Harry Bones said now.

"Said so in her letter. I figure the letter got here just one stage ahead of her," offered Felix. "What about all three of us meeting her?" he went on, suddenly thinking of the idea. "That would be good. What the hell, the woman didn't do anything. And I think we could at least be civil to her."

"Nobody's not being civil," Doc Joyner cut in. "But you men—as marshal and councilman of Sunshine Wells—are the ones to perform this duty. I—in the performance of *my* duties— attempt to heal the sick, not the bereaved."

"You both know how Torb Mill paid for the funeral."

"I don't guess anyone in this town doesn't know it," the doctor commented sardonically. "A gesture of compassion for the widow, obviously; not for the corpse," he added.

A sigh fell from the lips of Felix Porterhouse. "After all, compassion has to be in the air. Ephraim Crosby was our best-loved citizen, the finest man this little town has ever known, our benefactor, a father to many of us for the matter of that."

A low whistle, more like a simple movement of air, escaped the lips of Doctor Fabio Joyner as his bushy eyebrows rose high on his forehead and his eyes looked desperately toward the ceiling of the small office.

"I will meet the stage then," Felix said. "She reckoned she'd be on the noon stage today."

"Good luck then," Doc Joyner said as they went out.

On the boardwalk outside the office, Felix tried again. "Sure you wouldn't want to accompany me, Harry? You'll be watching the stage come in anyway, won't you?"

"That's part of my job; and I want to look the lady over beforehand. That don't mean I have to actually meet her."

And not waiting for Porterhouse to answer, the marshal of Sunshine Wells turned on his worn bootheel and started down the street, limping slightly, as Felix noted, from an old arrow wound taken up near Medicine Gap a good twenty years ago. A gift from the Shoshone.

Sunshine Wells lay at the edge of a long dish of land that ran from the foothills of the Absorokas down to the Greybull, the river tumbling across the land like a lazy lariat.

This was cattle country, far from the shipping points such as Ellsworth, Abilene, or Dodge City. Sunshine

Wells had never been written on a map; still it was there, a backwater town. Years ago, a massacre of the Indians by white religious fanatics had taken place here; and some old-timers now and again referred to it, though quietly, as if not really wanting to be heard, yet unable to forget it; or perhaps feeling something still in the atmosphere. Sunshine Wells was not a happy place. And the wretched murder of its most prominent citizen had not helped its quality of life.

The Gunsmith and Duke had left the company of the stage when they came within sight of the town and had ridden in independently. Their first stop had been Hoke's Livery at the far end of town. Here, under the gimlet gaze of the hostler, a man with enormous ears lying flat to his long head, Clint Adams stabled Duke and his team and gunsmithing wagon.

"That's a hoss you got there, mister." The words came gargling out of the man's wrinkled throat, while his Adam's apple pumped up and down a couple of times, and he scratched his buttocks vigorously with both hands.

"Then you'll take good care of him," Clint said, "and my team."

"Looks like gunsmithing," the hostler said. "You that feller I have heerd about, I reckon. But that's your business, not mine," he added quickly and turned away.

"Does this town have a hotel?" Clint asked, appreciating the oldster's way of covering himself while still trying to pry information.

"There is the Drover's Rest." And he nodded his head in the right direction. "Your hoss, your hosses, is in good hands, mister."

"I always expect the best and get it," the Gunsmith said warmly. "A man relies on his horse in this country."

"I'll be bound he better," the hostler said.

With a not unfriendly nod, yet a nod that signified he did expect the best, Clint Adams walked out of the livery.

The Drover's Rest was at the other end of town, so on his way there he had the opportunity to study the layout and the people and to speculate on how he might drum up some gunsmithing business. For Clint had come to Sunshine Wells for no other purpose than his chosen trade. In the back of his mind was a not-yet-formed notion to head eventually for the Sweetwater. And he had decided on Sunshine Wells as a layover on his way. Besides that, he'd never been here before. He was curious, having heard the place was out-of-the-way and not very friendly to strangers and run by a kindly old man with an iron fist.

The Gunsmith's hobby and livelihood centered on gunsmithing; but he was at the same time fascinated by people and their ways in handling one another and dealing with the raw life of the frontier. Yet there was something nagging at him as he walked up Main Street. He was not too happy about the hostler recognizing him as "the Gunsmith" for it was a name and reputation he wished had never been attached to him. The eastern journals and newspapers had coined it; always looking for excitement to stimulate their readers and separate them from their money. Well, his friend Wild Bill had had the same problem. Others, too. But Hickok had paid for his reputation with the ultimate—a bullet in the back.

The man at the desk of the Drover's Rest didn't make any comment when he read the name that the Gunsmith signed in the register—Clint Adams—but he did take a second look as he handed over the room key.

"You must be the one who saved the noon stage," he observed. "Good to have you about."

Clint nodded, but deliberately didn't look at the room clerk. "Just passing through."

"Stay as long as you like, mister. It ain't every day this town gets visitors such as the Gunsmith."

But the words fell on the Gunsmith's back as he turned and walked toward the stairs and his room. There was nothing he could do about it, he knew that, had known it ever since the rumors had started with the first newspaperman's story. Well, at least so far he wasn't getting talked about as much as Bill Hickok and some others he knew. So he dropped it. No point in chewing such a thing. Ruminating was for cows.

As Clint walked downstairs and into the lobby, he found several people entering the dining room. He was about to walk over and check the register to see if the dark-haired beauty from the stage was stopping there, when all at once he saw her in the mirror behind the desk clerk's head.

She was still dressed in mourning as she came very slowly down the stairs.

"Would you give me the pleasure of joining me?" Clint asked, going up to her.

"Ah, yes, the gallant gentleman from the stagecoach and Indian attack. Thank you." And she allowed him to conduct her into the dining room, where a waitress gave them a table to themselves.

"To my surprise, I'm quite hungry," she confided as she sat down.

The waitress took their order, and Clint watched the rather tired smile coming to the edges of his companion's wide mouth. He thought her lips were lovely.

Suddenly she said, "I realize you don't know who I am; even my name. I'm Jacqueline Gandy. As you see, I'm not exactly dressed for socializing. I hope you don't mind my accepting your kind offer. I'm—I'm afraid I'm not very good company."

And to his dismay he saw the tears spring to her eyes.

At that point Clint wanted nothing more than to take her in his arms and comfort her, and it was an effort to control himself.

"Look, why don't you tell me about it," he suggested. "Sometimes it helps to talk things out."

She was looking down at her hands. He could see that she had control of herself and would be all right. He saw her head nod, and when she looked up at him she was completley composed.

"Yes," she said. "You're right. I wonder . . ."

"Wonder what?" he asked as the waitress brought their order.

"I wonder . . . maybe you could help me." And then suddenly her mood changed. "But let's eat first, otherwise this fine-looking meal will get cold. And you should eat. I can tell you lead a very physical life; outdoors all the time and all that."

Clint realized that she was making a good attempt at

lifting her spirits, and he went along with it. And as they ate their steaks and potatoes and hominy he felt a great warmth for her. And so, as they had their meal, he let the talk flow as it would, not touching on anything serious, but letting the light moment heal something for her.

He ordered wine. It was good. It warmed him, and he knew it was doing the same for Jacqueline Gandy. Only he knew, too—and damn well—that it wasn't the wine that was making her more beautiful. And he suddenly remembered the old saw about widowhood making certain women more lovely. But he was sure that the young woman sitting across the table from him had been equally beautiful before her tragedy had struck. Whatever it was, he had no desire to be anywhere else but exactly where he was—listening to, looking at, feeling the very presence of this woman who had suddenly appeared in his life.

These days were the hottest of that early summer following the murder of Ephraim Crosby. The flaming sun reached deep into the land, burning along the stems of buffalo grass surrounding the town, all the way down to the roots. Like a fire it heated the tawny-colored earth, drew ripe sweat from man and horse, while the town dogs lay prone with panting tongues.

The sun was everywhere, waiting just outside the meager shade of the town's porches, pressing into the frame houses, numbing the life of the town. There was no escape. Nobody expected any. Some aged citizen, loaded with years of frontier sagacity, announced that it was the hottest summer in memory. Someone else—

an octogenarian widow—opined that the heat was "inhuman."

Nor was it cool in Marshal Harry Bones's office. The lawman and his three companions sat about on the crude furniture: two backless wooden chairs, an up-ended crate, and an armchair, with one arm.

"I'll be talking to Torb," Harry Bones was saying. "He's coming by, wanted to know how the woman was settin' in town—how the town's been taking her."

"I already told him all that," Felix Porterhouse cut in. "Can't see what else there's to mention."

All heard the whine in Porterhouse's voice, but they were so used to it, none made any comment either silently or aloud. Felix was always complaining about his place, why he wasn't given more importance, why he always had to do "all the dirty work."

"Hell, I told him how I met the woman at the depot, took her up to the Drover's; and let me tell you men again—as I've already told all of you-all—that Mrs. Gandy is a shrewd thing. Smart as a whip. Oh, sure—a widow, all busted up over her husband; even though he was, is, a murderer. But a man can't help feeling sorry for her."

"Nothin' to do with her bein' exceptional good-looking, is it, Felix?" Doc Joyner inquired wryly, bringing a titter of laughter from the group.

Harry Bones belched softly in the direction of the gray cat which had entered from the back room without making a sound, and now sat on its haunches and studied a fly that was buzzing at the potbellied stove in the center of the office. "She'll surely be visitin' us all and each," the marshal said. And he cocked his eye in

the direction of the fourth man in the group—Bob
Belden, Sunshine Wells's lone lawyer.

"She did ask about a lawyer," said Felix Porterhouse, quick as always to establish his importance.
"And I mentioned Bob here."

Bob Belden, a man in his late forties with a goatee
beard, looked important enough to be a judge, Harry
Bones was thinking as he looked at him now. Belden
was always dressed in black broadcloth, including a
vest with a large gold chain crossing it, at the end of
which was an impressive-looking gold watch. Harry
Bones, who was given to such details, noticed how
Belden always cleared his throat as he took out the
watch and snapped open its lid with his big hands and
dropped his eyes to read the time of day.

The lawyer did so now, almost as though he'd received the signal from the marshal's fleeting thought.
Harry Bones was impressed by the coincidence but
didn't mention it.

"Yes," Belden was saying, "the lady will be handled with kid gloves or mitts, depending on her approach. I am not in the mood for sympathy toward our
first citizen's murderer."

"Nor are any of us!" chimed in Felix Porterhouse.

"And she'll more than likely visit our marshal,"
Belden said, throwing a bland glance in the direction of
Harry Bones. "But I do believe we are all in accord as
to how we shall handle the—uh—situation." He cleared
his loose throat and taking out his watch again, flipped
open the lid. Obviously time was important to him.

"I suspect the woman needs to find some way of
relieving her grief over what has happened," put in

Doc Joyner. "Sure, her husband was a crazed killer—at least as so many of us put it—but . . ."

"What do you mean—as so many put it!" The words broke loudly from Felix Porterhouse. "Look, Fabio, are you thinking—"

"I am not thinking anything," snapped Joyner. "I am only putting that comment in because I am not so sure that justice was done. But—but . . ." And he held up his hands to stay any objections, ". . . but I am by no means suggesting it was *not* done. I do feel—and you have all heard me say so—that there was a pretty damn fast rush to judgment. I stand on my view!" He coughed, turning his head in the direction of the gray cat which, still silent on its haunches, was regarding the group impassively.

"Well, she will be finding us," said the marshal. "No one has anything he cannot say to the lady, I'm sure. What did you do, Felix; offer your condolences or something like that?"

"No, I did not offer my condolences to the widow of a murderer; the murderer of Ephraim Crosby, no less! I asked her if I could be of any assistance to her, and told her who I was and my position on the town council."

"Good enough," said Harry Bones, letting the words slip into the room like a casual "Amen" at the end of a mechanical prayer.

A silence fell suddenly upon them all. The gray cat was the first to move out of the mood that had taken the room. His name was Steve, and now he placed a paw forward, then followed it with his other paw, stretching with tremendous pleasure, with his toes spread wide; then arched his back high and yawned. Finally, wrapped in his own presence, he walked silently out of the room. Doc Joyner, who had been watching, thought it a magnificent gesture.

"We will have to speak to Torb," Felix, ever the good servant, murmured.

"Torb is no doubt way ahead of it already," Doc Joyner said, while Felix frowned at the heavy cynicism in the man's voice.

"Good thing we got Torb Mill," Felix said. "With poor Ephraim gone." And his voice dropped several notches for the appropriate sanctity.

Harry Bones had leaned back in his amputated armchair, letting his eyes go to the ceiling as he addressed Porterhouse. "Felix, we all honor Ephraim Crosby; let there be no question on that. But I don't feel we need to be Sweet-Jesused on it."

"Now, Harry, you are the representative of the law in Sunshine Wells, as I have so frequently pointed out, and as such . . ."

But the rest of whatever it was Felix wanted to say was lost in the scraping of chairs and boots as the group rose and began leaving the marshal's office. Felix was the last to go; the marshal remaining, but standing now at the window, watching his visitors make their way down Main Street.

He was still standing there when Steve walked silently back into the room, and without looking to left or right, went straight toward the man at the window and rubbed his back against the handy trouser leg.

Harry Bones hardly noticed. He was thinking of

Millicent. It was just a year ago that Millicent had died, making him still the most recent widower in Sunshine Wells.

It was outrageous. And somehow Clint Adams had known it would be. Something had told him that this woman—this girl—was what he called an "innocent." Not that Jacqueline Gandy wasn't fully able to handle herself in the difficulties of life—he knew she was thoroughly capable—but that there was an honesty, a purity in her eyes, her carriage, in her very tone that struck him as rare indeed. She knew her husband was no murderer, no matter what anybody might claim. And she was no fool. But Clint Adams could see she'd been hurt badly. At the same time, she was not going to be bullied or fooled.

Her story came in short bursts, in a quiet, contained manner of speaking. Only twice did she almost let her emotions overtake her, but her control came swift and firm. He could do nothing but admire her.

"It—it was all so—sudden. It came right out of the blue! A letter from the town marshal at Sunshine Wells. Todd arrested for murder, and then shot and killed while trying to escape! It . . . it could not be! It simply *could not be!*"

She had started to raise her voice, but immediately controlled herself, as two heads at a nearby table turned.

"I'm sorry! I'm embarrassing you . . . I . . ."

"You're not doing anything but telling me your story, and I do want to hear it," Clint said firmly

"Well, I don't know the whole thing. Only that Todd

is dead.'' She lowered her eyes, biting her lower lip to hold in her pain.

''We don't have to talk anymore now if you don't want to. In fact, it would probably be better if we didn't.''

''There isn't anything more to say. I am here. I wrote back that I was coming. A man—Mr. Porterhouse— met the stage and helped me with my bag, brought me here.'' She paused, and a wry look came into her young face. ''I could feel the town, the people . . . they knew who I was. And you must have noticed when we walked into the dining room—they knew me also.''

She stopped suddenly, looking down at her hands, which were lying beside her dinner plate.

''Could . . . could you . . . no, I can't ask you that.'' She spoke with her eyes still down and did not raise her head.

''Could I help you? I'm already helping you,'' the Gunsmith said.

Then she looked up, quickly, her deep hazel eyes fully on him. ''How so? I don't understand.''

''I'm on your side,'' he explained. ''I believe your husband was innocent. I've no evidence, of course, but sometimes you can just know something is so.''

She kept her eyes on him while he said this, and now he saw her tears; but they didn't fall. ''Thank you, thank you, Mr. Adams.''

''Clint.''

''I'm Jackie.''

They were silent while the waitress brought coffee.

''It's a strange experience,'' she said then. ''Today— on the coach, when you were there—I'd never have believed that only some few hours later I'd be telling so much to a man I didn't know.''

"It's just between us," Clint said. "You needn't worry that anything you tell me will go any further."

"I'm not worried."

"It's going to be all right." But he wondered at his words.

"I should tell you why my husband had to travel out here in the first place."

"Take your time," Clint said. "I've got plenty of time, just to listen." He smiled at her and was gratified to detect the trace of something like a smile at the corners of her full mouth.

"Todd is . . . was . . . a lawyer. He dealt in land grants, I believe, though he never talked much about his work. Anyhow, he had to come out here to this place to settle a widow's estate; something like that. The widow lived in our town but owned property here, which had been left her when her husband died. She'd moved east as she got older and she also wanted to live with her daughter. Todd had been taking care of her affairs for two or three years. Anyhow, that's how he happened to visit Sunshine Wells." She took a sip of her coffee, then resumed. "That's all I know . . . until I got Marshal Bones's letter."

"Your husband didn't know anybody else in Sunshine Wells; I mean, he wasn't doing any other business here?"

"Not that I know of."

"Would he have told you?"

"I think so. As I say, I didn't know much about his

business, but he did tell me things now and again. I think Mrs. Wagner was the only business he had here."

"Looks to me, then, that while your husband came here minding his business, somebody else was also minding his business."

"I don't want to take advantage of your time," she said. "Your kindness.

And he replied, "Don't worry. I never waste my time. I always put my time to good use."

Then he escorted her out of the dining room and said good-night as she headed for the stairs leading to the rooms on the upper floor.

THREE

It didn't take him long to walk through the town after he had said good-bye to Jackie Gandy. Obviously, this was an overlooked town, barely functioning it seemed; or perhaps he was just reacting to the grim feeling he had about the fate of Todd Gandy.

He had noted almost everything there was to note about Sunshine Wells when he'd first arrived, and it was no different now with night cloaking the scene. Some parts of the boardwalk were in sore need of repair. Most of the fronts of the buildings lining Main Street were in need of paint. Loose shingles dangled from walls and rooftops, right on the edge of breaking free to land possibly on some passerby.

It was in the Screaming Eagle that Clint decided to begin his investigation. The saloon, the gambling hall, the barber, were always good places to put his ear to the ground.

"Town always this quiet?" he asked casually as he stood at the bar with his first glass of beer.

The bartender, a man of wide girth and thin eyebrows had been wiping the mahogany around Clint's glass.

"Usually quiet, but it's more so, I do admit it." He nodded at Clint's half empty glass. "Put some salt in that if you want it; give it a good collar."

"It's all right as is."

"Figured you for a feller would know that much already," the barman said amiably, still wiping, his big hand buried in the damp cloth.

The Gunsmith was figuring that the man wanted to know more about him. It was usually the case when he came into a new town.

"I see the marshal's office is closed," Clint said.

"Wanted to see the marshal, did you?"

"Just to say how-de-do. Tell him I'm here with my gunsmithy shop, and he might steer me into the way of business. For the matter of that, you might." And Clint smiled a very friendly smile at the big man on the other side of the bar. The barman returned the grin, though a little sourly. "I quit that kind of life when I got busted up by a little pinto horse. I dee-cided then, cowboyin' was not the life for Zeke Wools."

The Gunsmith said nothing to that, letting his silence fill the gap. And Zeke Wools picked up on it.

"Got two big reasons, stranger. I am sayin' the why of the quiet. Not that we ain't kinda quiet anyways in Sunshine, but I know what you're meaning. Two big reasons," he repeated, and his hand stopped, and remained buried in the thick bar rag. "Two deaths. Two new graves in the cemetery, by God. You'll maybe see some flowers on the one, but for sure not on th'other."

"How come?" The Gunsmith kept his voice casual,

as though he was just moving the conversation along, not trying to seek out any information.

"The man practically founded this here town," the barkeep said. "Actually, it was Clyde Hossenden built the first shack and even gived his name to the town; used to be called Hossenden, but Ephraim, he had it changed to Sunshine Wells. I dunno why." He paused, and leaning back, directed a stream of spittle toward a hidden cuspidor in back of the bar.

"That was Ephraim Crosby?" Clint asked.

"Sure was. Ephraim Crosby, he grubstaked every new settler that come out here and it was himself was responsible for gettin' the town started. Much more'n Old Hoss. Hoss was a good man, but Ephraim Crosby, he really milked the cow, if you know what I mean. An' I reckon you do."

"Sounds like a good man; the both of them," Clint added. "Though this fellow Crosby, I've heard others speak highly of him."

" 'Course. 'Course . . ."

"Heard Crosby was killed."

"Murdered! Murdered in cold blood, by a cowardly son of a bitch!" Zeke Wools leaned forward, his hands flat on the mahogany bar, his big belly rolling over the edge. When he leaned back, taking a big breath to emphasize his words, Clint noticed that his white shirt was wet from leaning into the beer slops which had spread from his glass.

"Murdered! And now that poor Lilly Crosby; by golly, if she ain't the best-lookin', purtiest woman you ever did lay eyes on, now a widow. A widow, with her man six-feet deep; and all I can say is that by God so is

that goddam crazy boozed-up dude easterner what somehow or the other lured Ephraim out of his home that
night an' slid that knife into him. Christ almighty!''

"What was his name?" Clint asked.

"Gander—no, Gandy. Gandy was his name. Come
in on the five o'clock stage and by damn he never even
checked into the Drover's Rest where everybody—all
the travelers—stays. The mangy son of a bitch come
right here to the Screaming Eagle and started building
himself a drunk that'd put down a hoss, by God!''

"Sounds like he was thirsty," said Clint. But the
wry humor was lost on Zeke Wools.

"He put it away, I am telling you! Then, later—way
past midnight—Dutch got woked up by a yell outside
his room, outside his window; that's Dutch Bilder, the
swamper here at the Screaming Eagle; he's got a place
back of the building where he stays. So he gets up and
goes out and what does he see but Old Ephraim Crosby
flat on his back lyin' on the ground there, with a knife
in his chest and that goddam dude lyin' right there next
him. Out he was, having drunk enough to bring an
army regiment to its knees, and lyin' there with his
hand still on the handle of that knife that was stickin'
into Old Ephraim!''

The Gunsmith let a low, soft whistle escape through
his lips in appreciation of the storyteller's talent.

"I bet that Dutch set up to hollering loud enough to
raise the whole town," he said.

"You bet it!" The barkeep growled the words in
severe regard of the awesome moment. "That feller
was so drunk they had to carry him to the jail. By time
he come to he was locked in good. Not a man among us

figured he could make a break, or would even try it, such a damn fool thing. But by God, he did. He got out. 'Course that was a day later.''

"Did the man get his chance to tell his side of it?" Clint asked.

"Dunno about that, but there was never no trial," the bartender said. "That feller, Gander, Gandy—he knew he was a gone goose, knew for sure he'd stretch. Why would he of done what he done otherwise? Huh? Answer me that!"

"I don't know what he did," Clint said.

"Tricked Bones's deputy. Bert Smiles, not too bright, Bert. Claimed he needed drinking water, somethin' like that; maybe had to take a leak. I dunno. Doesn't matter." Zeke Wools sniffed, a long sniff, and loud as he warmed to his story, which surely had been honed, the Gunsmith realized, through many tellings since the event had occurred.

"Outsmarted Bert. Slick like a wolf, a goddam coyote, better; and poor Bert made the mistake of coming too close to the cell door."

"How did he get him?" Clint asked blandly.

"Got his hands on Bert, right around his throat, and with the other snaked Bert's hogleg out of its holster. Double-action Colt it was, in the hand of that murderer now. Got Bert to unlock his cell, then he pistol-whipped him and got out. But not plumb away. Not, by God, plumb away!"

He leaned his big hands on the bar and stood there, nodding his head in agreement with his own story.

"What happened? He did something dumb then?"

"He ran into Heavy John Bearing, him who runs the

Double Bar B, and three of his men." He paused, waving away a fly that was trying to land on his bulbous nose.

"Then?" the Gunsmith asked offhandedly.

Zeke spread his hands apart and shrugged elaborately. "Then they were all there, with the dude pointing Bert Smiles's Colt at 'em, and they, by God, drilled him, I mean right now!"

Suddenly, as if by cue, somebody called him from the end of the bar and he moved away.

Clint was in no hurry to finish his beer, so he stayed where he was, turning it all over in his mind; seeing clearly the setup. It was crazy. It had to be a setup. Gandy's card had been aced the minute he set foot in town.

Clint looked down the bar. Zeke was talking to some men at the other end. Well, he had plenty to think about, and he was just wondering whether he would order another beer when he heard a voice behind him.

"You don't have to look so dour, stranger . . ."

Turning, his eyes swept the youthful blonde who was standing there. She reminded him of a girl he'd encountered not too long ago in Denver. And that memory provoked him to turn his head toward Zeke and call for another round.

"What'll it be?" he asked the girl.

"You name it, mister," she answered, her eyes combing his face.

"We'll make it whiskey," he said as Zeke the bartender came up. And he felt the familiar stirring in his trousers as the girl's smile broadened, softened, and she moved closer.

•   •   •

The room was small, but the bed was large. It seemed to Clint Adams that actually the room was all bed. It had been a long time and the girl was just what he needed.

"You're just what I needed," he said after their satiated bodies had rested a few moments, as they lay side by side on their backs.

"Likewise," the blonde girl said, and she brought her leg over his waist, pushing her womanhood against his side.

"That feels good."

"I want more."

"There's more where that came from."

"You know something? You want to know something?"

"Yeah? What?" he asked.

"The minute I got a look at you downstairs in the bar I knew you were the kind who never had to pay for it. Funny—huh?"

"You know something?"

"Yeah?"

"I knew it, too." And he turned toward her, his erection at its full rigidity again, as she spread her legs for him.

"I like it that you take your time."

"It's the best way," he answered, as he rolled on top of her and pushed all the way in as far as he could go.

"Oh, oh, oh!" First the word came on her breath, then louder, and again louder, until he closed her mouth with his, slipping his tongue deep into her, while their bodies began their delicious rhythm.

Now she brought her legs up high, almost onto his

shoulders as she bucked with him, rutting together like two happy animals in another time, another place. He thought he would go crazy with joy.

Now they rode faster, and without missing a stroke he worked her over onto her hands and knees so that he was mounting her from the rear, his hands reaching forward to squeeze her hanging breasts, which were as soft and firm as any he had ever encountered. She was gasping, squealing with total delight as they raced in perfect harmony to their climax.

"My God, it's quarts, gallons you're giving me. My God!" She breathed the words into his ear as he squirted and squirted again and again; it seemed endlessly into her soaking, pumping vagina.

They lay entwined like two exhausted rags, soaking in their love juice, their lungs pumping for air, their bodies quivering with the ecstasy that had totally claimed them; and still did.

Then they slept.

They did it a third time and slept again.

"You're the best, mister," she said, watching him as he got dressed.

"My name's Clint. What's yours?"

"Angie, but you can call me any name you like."

"I've always favored Angie."

"I'd like to see you again."

"I'm not stopping you." He was buckling his belt.

"Well, you know where I am," she said. "Just remember the old saying—practice makes perfect."

He grinned at her, his eyes taking in her totally naked

body, with her belly shiny from their mutual exertions. "Let's not try to get perfect," he said.

"Why? Why not?"

"It's much more fun to keep practicing," the Gunsmith said as he bent down and kissed her slowly.

"I see what you mean," she said, her eyes still closed. She was still lying on her back and in the next moment she reached up and began opening his fly.

Clint thought his knees were getting pretty weak, and for a moment he didn't know whether to sit down or remain standing. In the next instant he realized there was no question about what he was going to do.

She suddenly sat up, and swinging her legs around, straddled his knees as he stood beside the bed. She pulled out his rigid organ—with some difficulty, but successfully.

"I want to eat him this time," she said.

"But lying down," he said.

She mumbled something. He couldn't hear her reply, for she had his penis halfway down her throat and was sucking and licking it all the way.

"Double tragedy it was," Harry Bones was saying to his visitor, Clint Adams.

"It's especially rough on the widows," the Gunsmith put in, just carrying the conversation. He had dropped by the marshal's office simply to inform him he was in town, having missed him on his first try. Bones had heard of him, Clint could tell, but it seemed to make no difference to the marshal. Clint was glad for this. Sometimes he ran into lawmen who were feisty about the Gunsmith appearing in their town, and sometimes he ran into the awestruck, the devotees of the fast gun. Harry Bones was neither. In fact, as Clint put it to himself, the marshal of Sunshine Wells appeared grown-up.

"Help yerself to more arbuckle there," Bones said, nodding toward the coffeepot on the jumbo stove. "Ain't too hot. Didn't want to build a new fire with all this heat already about." He leaned back in his armchair with one arm and pushed his hat back on his head.

"Obliged," Clint replied, helping himself, while he felt Steve the cat's eyes upon him. He had already asked the marshal about the killing of Ephraim Crosby and also about Todd Gandy's escape. Nothing new came out of it. Yet he still felt there was more. Somewhere. Not necessarily more facts, was how he put it to himself, but rather a more open view of the situation, a clearer sight of the connections, and of course, there were the things that were unsaid. For instance, no one seemed to have wondered what the old man had been doing out in the street so late at night. All had maintained that Crosby was no carouser.

But while Harry Bones was obviously a man who knew himself pretty well, his deputy was another matter. Clint ran into Smiles in the Screaming Eagle later the same day.

"Beats me why Gandy's widow'd want to come out to Sunshine Wells anyway," the deputy had said, frowning.

"Her man's buried here," Clint pointed out. "Seems to me a good enough reason."

"The murderer!"

"You sure?" Clint asked mildly. They were standing

at one end of the bar and nobody was nearby, so their conversation was quite private.

"No offense," Bert Smiles said hastily, rubbing his fat palm over his lumpy red face. "But I reckon it is hard for the lady to believe—huh?"

"Too hard, I'd say," the Gunsmith said, finding it hard not to indulge his dislike of the man he was talking to. "She was his wife. They had to be close. If she felt he was the kind of man who would do such a thing, she wouldn't have come out here in the first place."

"Loyal, I reckon," Bert said, sucking his teeth and sniffing. "But Gandy was guilty. I mean—guilty!"

And suddenly his face flushed, he slapped his hand down on the bar, and without another word turned and walked out of the saloon.

"You got him riled some, I'd say."

The voice at his elbow brought Clint's head around.

"Doc Joyner," said the tall man who had just moved in beside him. "You—I take it—are Clint Adams."

Clint nodded, waiting to see if the other would mention that he was also the Gunsmith, as so often happened. To his relief, Doc Joyner refrained.

Instead, the doctor said, "I hope you've got your tools with you, Adams. I have a single-action Colt, which I rarely use, and a Henry that both need work. Would you have time?"

"Sure would. Got my wagon down at the livery and I'll come by. Where are you located?"

"Main Street." He pointed the direction with his thumb. Then he said, "I heard about you helping the coach out by Jolly Butte."

"Wasn't much trouble. Those Indians were pretty well liquored. I mean, about half paralyzed."

"Sure enough somebody's been selling 'em the whiskey," Doc Joyner said. "They're a small band, but they've been making trouble some while now." He shook his head, his jowls quivering slightly. He was a man in his late fifties, still vigorous, still with the glint of humor in his eye. "Could lead to big trouble."

"Would you know of any reason why Gandy would kill Ephraim Crosby?" Clint asked, deciding now on a frontal approach, as he sized up the doctor.

Joyner's eyebrows lifted in query, he shrugged, looked at his glass of whiskey, and then looked at the Gunsmith.

"I don't think he even knew Crosby," Clint went on. "Fact, he likely didn't know anybody in town, only the widow Wagner, and she wasn't living here anymore."

"I wondered some about it myself," Joyner said, lowering his voice and moving closer to Clint. "Let's sit over there," he said, nodding in the direction of a vacant table near the far wall.

When they were seated, away from the general buzz of conversation around the bar and the card tables, Clint returned to his questioning.

"Do you know what time his stage got in; Gandy's?"

"Likely five. If it was on time. Isn't always; but I'd say five, give or take. But could be six."

"The point is, he gets into town late afternoon, heads straight here to this place, takes on a load of booze. Did you by any chance see him?"

Joyner was shaking his head. "No. But I of course heard—as everybody did—that he had a real snootful.

When they found him they had to carry him to the jail. I mean he was drunk!''

"But you didn't actually see him yourself."

"Nope. I did hear he was drinking the good stuff, not trail whiskey. He was drinking fine bourbon. Torb Mill has it freighted in from Cheyenne."

"So he was feeling and acting pretty numb by the time the place here closed; stumbling drunk and hardly able to keep his eyes open is how I've heard it."

"That is how I heard it, too," Doc Joyner said agreeably.

"Yet he suddenly finds himself strong enough to jump an old man and stick a knife right through his heart. And—mind you—I have been told he never even carried a knife. I'd like somebody to think about that, and then tell me why somebody else couldn't have killed Crosby."

Clint had been letting his voice rise as he continued to speak, with the intention of attracting some of the men in the saloon. He was thinking it would be the only way he might catch an opposing opinion to the assumed open-and-shut guilt of Todd Gandy.

Right now a fresh voice entered the conversation. He had felt somebody coming closer to their table but had refrained from looking up, letting the man think he was cutting in unexpectedly.

"It's not possible," said the new voice. "No other strangers in town except the other passengers, who were by then all asleep. And by God, no Sunshine Wells man would harm a hair of Ephraim Crosby's head. You can stand on that!''

It was a long, sloping man who had approached. He

was shaped like a pear, with wide hips, small feet, and pointed hands. Even his head seemed to come to a point.

"Are you suggesting Ephraim Crosby was some kind of a saint?" Clint asked.

"Ephraim was everybody's saint, or benefactor if you like," the pear-shaped man said. "Me—in case you want to know, stranger—I run this place for Ephraim, well, for his widow now."

"You're Boyd Harrigan," Clint said, and he held out his hand. "Pleased to meet you. I'm Clint Adams."

"You're the. . . ." But he stopped and changed his whole stance suddenly, "Yeah . . . pleased to meet you, Adams."

"It's true, Adams," Doc Joyner said. "Ephraim Crosby helped a whole lot of people in this town. I can't speak for myself in that respect, but I do know he helped others."

"Helped us all to get started, Fabio," Harrigan said. "You, 'course, come here with your shingle . . . medicine . . . you didn't need any help."

"I could use a little help in getting some of the folks around to pay their bill," Joyner said wryly, and cut a shrewd wink at Clint Adams.

"Ephraim helped me get started, by golly," Boyd Harrigan went on. "Me, the storekeepers, and the local cattlemen hereabouts. This ain't a rich town, but by God, people got a roof over their heads. And it was Crosby got the money for to build these homes. Sure he collected rent, and even now and again somebody claimed as how the rent was too high, but that didn't happen often. Ephraim was tough, but he was fair."

"Sounds like a nice man," Clint remarked blandly.

A man who had been standing nearby now joined the group, taking the pipe out of his mouth as he did so.

"I got me a wife, a mother-in-law, and two kids," he said. "An' if it hadn't been for Ephraim Crosby renting me a place out on the south fork, I'd be shacking it, or worse."

"This here," Boyd Harrigan said, cutting in swiftly, "this saloon. He owned it, plus others in town, and the stores, and the Drover's Rest. I helped with the managing. Worked closely with Torb Mill, who was really Crosby's right-hand man. Well, hell, Ephraim collected; he wasn't a damn fool when it came to turning a profit; why should he be? But he always gave us a fair return."

"So who'll be running things now?" Clint asked casually. "Torb Mill?"

"No, no," Boyd Harrigan cut in swiftly. "We'll be speaking to Lilly now; she's the widow. I expect she'll run things about like Ephraim did; likely with Torb assisting."

The whole point as far as Clint could see was that just about everybody in town was indebted to Ephraim Crosby; the town's most important, most popular citizen. And the most feared? The question kept nagging him long after he parted company with the little group of men in the Screaming Eagle.

Meanwhile, he had become well aware of the fact that somebody had been—and still was—following him as he moved about the town. It wasn't long before he realized it was the little man he had seen in the stagecoach seated next to Jackie Gandy.

•   •   •

Abner Frolicher, a hardly noticeable man, thin, wizened beyond his actual years, would never have
admitted—even to himself—that life had always held
the whip hand as far as he was concerned. Abner had
been fired from three newspapers for incompetence,
had also failed as a gambler, a hawker of medical
nostrums, and—not so finally—as a lover. He was
neither handsome nor sufficiently ugly to be found
attractive by the opposite sex. His was a dubious record
at best by the time he had reached his thirtieth year,
which was the present.

At thirty he found himself with no family; his wife
had left him after three years of, as she'd put it, "mari-
tal boredom," his parents and immediate relatives
lived—he presumed—in Pennsylvania. He did not cor-
respond with his past. And perhaps his one positive
characteristic—were anyone to take the time to consider
him as a subject for thought or conversation—was that
he did keep trying. In fact, Abner lived in the future—
that is to say, his dreams of greatness, popularity, and
at least moderate wealth. But mostly Abner was lonely.
He envisioned success as the cure for this sometimes
hardly bearable pain. In a word, he longed for popularity, to at least be liked.

The secret of his failure—and he would never, never
have admitted it—was that he was afraid of people. He
had reason to be, having been beaten to a pulp more
times than he could remember by his parents when he
was a small boy, a mere child. Abner Frolicher was
unloved, unlovable; but he did have one thing of value;
determination ran through him like gold through the
Comstock.

Upon realizing that the Gunsmith was going to be in the very town he was visiting—in the hope of finding a job on the local newspaper—Abner was overjoyed. His dream became again possible. He would write the true story of this fabulous man of the fabulous West—the swiftest, most accurate, most successful gunslinger of them all. An eastern publisher would pay plenty for such a story. Why, it might even become a book! Not only money but literary fame would be his dessert!

Abner had done a lot of reading in his time—one of the acceptable panaceas for loneliness—and this new possibility suggested a whole new career. Not only a book, but lecture tours, invitations to meet the literati, romance!

And so he set about his new career in his usual pedestrian way: by following the subject about town, making notes—mostly mentally—on who, what, when, where, and even why the subject was talking to so many people: barber, blacksmith, bartender, doctor, saloon swamper, even one of the girls who plied her trade at the Screaming Eagle. And he realized that his subject—his quarry—was a shrewd man, knowing who the loose mouths were in town.

At the same time, Abner had begun to feel uneasy, for the more he tried to follow and watch the Gunsmith, the more he began to realize that the man knew he was being watched. What worried him now at this very moment was the fact that his quarry had made no move toward him. Was the Gunsmith plotting some unspeakable disaster that would suddenly be sprung on him in total surprise? When excitement of this nature overtook Abner he usually began to tremble inside, which nobody but himself could know about, but also his lower lip would quiver slightly, and saliva would collect at the corners of his mouth. This was doing so now as he saw the Gunsmith crossing the street at dusk, heading for the Cabbage Patch; obviously with the purpose of quizzing some of the ladies known as ''soiled doves.''

Abner stood just inside the alley that ran along one side of the bank and watched. Surely it would be better now to come out in the open and speak to the Gunsmith, asking him for his cooperation; and thus not only get some rich, much-needed material on the man, but also in order to allay any hostility from that quarter. But Abner didn't want to. Abner was afraid, although he put it to himself that he was being discreet, careful, patient, that the moment wasn't precisely ''ripe'' for confrontation, that speaking too soon might foil his whole plan, etcetera, etcetera. Meanwhile, from the alley next to the bank, he watched the Gunsmith disappear into the gloom that had now enveloped the Cabbage Patch.

FOUR

"That's him; that's the Gunsmith."

Felix Porterhouse said those words without taking his eyes off the figure going quickly down the other side of Main Street.

The big man standing beside him said, "There is no doubt in your mind."

Felix turned toward Torb Mill in surprise. "Doubt? It's him! No question."

"There are fakers about," Mill said. "Men trying to make it on somebody else's hard work. I want you to be sure."

"I am sure. And so is Harry Bones. Harry used to be a big lawman some years back. He wouldn't be fooled."

Torb Mill said nothing, just stood there, watching Clint Adams disappear from sight as evening sifted into the town. He was a dour man, with a face that looked as though it had been carved rather carelessly. A man who took up a lot of space, though he wasn't actually very large. His eyes, straddling his hawklike nose, were a piercing blue. They were the kind of eyes that took what they saw. A man in his fifties, immaculately dressed in black broadcloth, he now held an expensive Havana in the fingers of his left hand.

"He is somebody we could use," Torb Mill said. And he moved closer to the window, crowding Felix out of his position, to the latter's great irritation.

"Don't know if he can be trusted," Porterhouse said, trying to regain ground.

"Hell, nobody with any sense would trust anybody. Don't you know that?"

"Man's got to trust somebody, something," Felix insisted.

"Only a damn fool trusts. Listen: 'Trust nobody but yourself, then you've got no one else to blame.' " He intoned the last words, as though quoting verbatim. Which maybe he was.

"He's a man we could use," Mill repeated. "Locate him. I want to see him. Then I'll know what I want to do."

Felix Porterhouse nodded. Then he said, "Matter of fact, that fellow—Adams, his real name is—was the one who drove off those drunken Injuns who hit the noon stage; I'm talking about the stage that brought the woman to town."

"Gandy? The wife?"

"That's it."

"You're saying he might have spoken with her, maybe even have gotten close. He might have heard things from her."

"Right. She might have turned him toward her way of looking at things—that her husband was innocent, didn't kill Crosby."

"Obviously she's here in an attempt to clear his name. Or maybe only to pay respects to his grave. Or both. But get that fellow Adams for me."

"I don't think he'll be much help to us," Felix said, still trying not to be swept under by the aggressiveness of the man he worked for.

"Look, I am not interested in getting him to help us—or me. Me," he repeated. "I am concerned that he does *not* help the woman. Now do you get it?"

And his hard marble eyes stared down at the shorter man.

Felix Porterhouse's face had flushed russet right up through his hairline. He was furious at the way Mill always managed to set him down.

The number-one man on the town council had already turned away, and now crossed the room to his big desk and sat down, his hand already reaching for papers as he puffed at the big cigar he held between his teeth.

It was clear to Felix Porterhouse that the meeting was over, that Torb Mill had dismissed him—that once again the number-one man on the council had aced number two.

The enormous figure that opened the door had to be the proprietress; that is, the Madam. No one else could have filled that body, supported the incredible shock of dyed orange hair, the double chin, the great cheeks, the bulging neck so thickly, so fragrantly rice-powdered. She was rouged, her lips were painted, while the great pillows that were her breasts were barely covered by the loose kimono of the most extraordinary colors. Between her fat fingers, captured by a host of rings, was a cold stogie.

"What can I do you for, honey?" The voice came from a bed of gravel as she lifted the cigar butt to her flaming lips and raised her eyebrows. "Got a light, have you?"

The Gunsmith obliged, taking a lucifer from his shirt pocket and holding the light for her.

Through the resulting cloud of stinging smoke, her words came to inform him that the establishment had just acquired some new girls, that prices had *not* gone up, and that what was offered the honest, clean customer was "the best in the West."

"You can call me Sophie," she said, her voice taking on a note of regality. "I run this here place." While she was speaking, she had moved back inside the house, drawing him in as though by a magnet.

"I'm not looking for any sport right now, Sophie," Clint said. "Just have some questions I'd like to ask you."

Immediate suspicion invaded the powdered face. "I don't know anything about my girls except they're each and every one honest as the day is long; and they are clean. And that's the God's honest truth, so help me!" She held up her hand as though swearing on the Good Book, with her cigar butt clasped between her fingers.

Still, as he smiled warmly at her she gave ground and led him into the parlor, a not very tidy room rank with the odors of tobacco, booze, and cheap perfume.

"I can offer you a drink, my friend," she said.

"Not right now, thanks, but I'll be back," he added.

"Huh." She glared at him malevolently, her cigar

clutched in her jaws. He noticed that she had the suspicion of a mustache. "We'll believe that when we see it."

Clint decided then that he would come right to the point. People like Sophie were often more trustworthy than the so-called respectable citizens, for the simple reason that they were socially outside and thus could afford to think and feel more freely than their constricted brothers and sisters.

"I'm just in town here for a short spell, but I'm a friend of this fellow Gandy's widow. You probably know she's in town."

The eyes stared at him like two stones.

"I've been talking with her, listening to her, and I'm trying to get the story of what happened to her husband so's she'll go on back home feeling maybe a little easier about things."

"I reckon it throwed her—huh?"

"It sure did. And she is still thrown," Clint said. "She doesn't take it that her husband stuck a knife in Crosby. But if you don't feel free to talk to me, that's all right. I am not going to push you."

"I am damn well free to talk to who I like and when I like." The words came snapping back at him and he had to grin. "In this town, by damn, Sophie O'Govern don't give a good or a bad goddam what anybody thinks. The men is men and as long as they pay their money—cash on the barrel head—I got me a business. The law ain't gonna close me down. Not Harry Bones. He ever tried that, he'd get run out of town on a rail. But hell, this town, there is no secrets that everybody doesn't already know about anyways. Everybody knows everybody else's business—I mean from zero to zero. Now then—'' She leaned forward with her elbow on one knee, the cigar between her ringed fingers, and regarded her visitor coldly. ''What do you want to know?''

''I want to ask you about the night of the jailbreak; I understand there were a couple of Double Bar B men in the place here.''

''They were here a good while; came early, stayed late. Jesse Ollinger and Dink Wilson.''

''Anybody else happen by?''

''Their boss showed up around . . . I'd say around two, it was.'' She nodded in memory of the particular time. ''Yeah, right around two o'clock.''

''Was he alone?''

''Had another man with him.''

''That's Bearing, is it?''

''Heavy John. Right. He come for Ollinger and Wilson. Yeah. . . . Wanted them for an early start. They were pushing the herd up onto the mountain that next day; something like that. I didn't but half hear any of it on account of I wasn't 'specially listening.''

''So Bearing got them, that making three plus himself, and took off. Right?''

''Right.''

''And then, a bit later there was the shooting. I understand it wasn't so far from here. You heard it?''

''Sure did. Up the alley there, that runs past the back of this place. That Gandy fellow, it appears they ran into him.''

The Gunsmith nodded. ''Yeah. . . . That's about how I heard it. Just wanted to make sure, so I thought I'd check with you. You have the reputation of being a straight shooter.''

He had added that last because he had in fact heard that, but also to mollify any doubts in her mind as to why he was questioning the situation.

Sophie looked at him with her lip curled as though she wanted to spit, but then her face relaxed, even softened somewhat. And the Gunsmith saw beneath the surface of the tough madam. He saw someone a good deal younger, someone who had indeed had a hard life. No, not someone with a ''heart of gold'' as he knew the eastern writers sometimes put it about the wild women of the western towns and hamlets, but a person who threw a clean loop. He liked Sophie, and the equal fact of that, he soon saw, was that she liked him, too.

''You're that Gunsmith feller, I have heard of you. Well, you don't look too bad to me. Fact, I might give you some time myself, not throw you to some of these inexperienced young kids I got here. A man like you needs someone with that extra—if you follow my drift—someone who knows the difference between up and down. You follow my drift, do you?''

''I appreciate your offer,'' Clint said with a sinking feeling. ''But I'm pretty well tied up right now. Maybe. . . .''

''Got your cap set for that new widow, I'll be bound,'' said Sophie. ''Men—I know how you'll bet 'em 'fore you look at 'em, Mr. Gunsmith. Well, you don't know what you're missing here. But think it over. Think it over.''

And she was still telling him to think it over as she

walked him to the front door and let him out of the house.

The barroom wasn't crowded, but there were a good dozen customers when Clint Adams walked in. Four cowhands were lining the bar, drinking shots of whiskey along with beer—boilermakers.

Clint walked to the far end of the bar and ordered a beer. He had come in on the spur of the moment, thinking it might again be time to get the feel of the town—the gossip, the vibration of how the town was feeling his presence as well as Jacqueline Gandy's.

Those four he noted were rough-looking boys, and their mouths were loud. The men from the town were not a part of their gaggle, which was growing louder and more pointed as the Gunsmith slowly drank his beer.

Zeke Wools had ambled back to where Clint was standing, seeming to lean on the bar, but actually with his body free and ready for any fast moves.

"Double Bar B waddies," the barkeep said warily when Clint moved his eyes questioningly in their direction. "Don't ask me their names, an' watch yerself."

Clint saw instantly that the four were on the prod, more so now as their voices rose even higher, to include the whole barroom.

"Only a man lowern' whale shit'd be takin' up with that widow of a murderin' son of a bitch," said the biggest of the four. They were all big, but this man was over six feet; and he had a voice to match his body. Not one of them could have been much more than twenty, twenty-five, Clint saw. He continued to sip his beer quietly at his end of the bar, but he knew they were working up to a showdown.

Boyd Harrigan was seated near the back of the room, frowning, but obviously keeping himself under control. He had no wish for his saloon to be wrecked by a bunch of randy cowpokes who were only a little more than dry behind the ears. At the same time, they were Heavy John Bearing's boys; and Heavy John, as he and a lot of others in town well knew, had his "ways."

A long, wiry man spoke up now. "That son of a bitch didn't have the guts to stick it out for a fair trial. The bugger had to go and bust outta jail and so he got just what he deserved."

"Hell, he got off easy," said a third. "Jesse, it was a damn good thing you and Dink cut the son of a bitch down. He was a killer, no two ways of lookin' at it. You done the town a service."

The fourth man, Jesse, grinned. He was lean, hard, but at the same time sinewy—a whip. He wore his six-gun tied low on his right thigh.

At that point the swinging doors opened and Abner Frolicher walked in. Abner regretted it instantly as his eyes took in the pregnant tableau that was rapidly shifting into hard focus. But it was too late. Abner realized he had to play it easy but firmly. Afraid he was—of people, yes—but he had that underlying determination that had often led him into trouble in the past, and which he was afraid would also lead him now. Yet, he knew it as a determination—a fear, he had once figured—a fear that was afraid of showing fear. And so he walked to the bar, taking a place—and to his own astonishment—about halfway between Clint Adams and the four cowboys. It wasn't at all easy to keep his voice steady as he ordered a whiskey.

Nor was it so simple a matter to carry glass and bottle to a table at the back of the room with steady legs. But he made it. As he sat down he almost sighed aloud with relief. And in a strange way his astonishment stayed with him; he realized he had probably never felt this good in his life. At the same time, he knew he had to be extra careful. He was out of any line of fire, and he had a close-up seat to the action; but he didn't want in any way to be included in an exchange of lead.

The Gunsmith was still standing easy all by himself as the lean, whiplike cowboy named Jesse said, "There is some in town who thinks that wasn't the fair and right thing to do—saving the hangman his work, and in a way, taking the bread out of the poor feller's mouth." He was looking directly at the Gunsmith now, his eyes hard, glinting with his goading humor.

Clint Adams knew exactly what was coming, but he didn't move. And now he lifted his glass of beer slowly to take a drink—with his right hand. He knew exactly what he was going to do. It was definitely time to bring things to a head.

"Jesse, that's enough. Cool down and leave it be," said Boyd Harrigan from near the back of the room.

"Mind your own business, Harrigan," snapped Jesse.

"This is my place and my business. Now you mind yourself," said Harrigan getting up from his chair. He was unarmed, but the man had courage.

"I hear this man's been asking a lot of questions around town about what happened," the young cowpoke said, his lips twisted in a sneer. "Also been dancin' attendance on that murderer's widow, I bin told."

Clint was still holding his beer glass in his right hand as Jesse squared off, his hand dropping closer to his gun side.

"By God, Jesse, if you pull a gun in this saloon you'll never get another drink here, so help me!"

But Jesse was ignoring Boyd Harrigan; his eyes were boring into the Gunsmith, who still held his beer half-way to his mouth, was still leaning—or so it seemed—against the bar. Behind the bar, Zeke Wools had frozen.

The room was suddenly silent.

Abner Frolicher, his heart pounding, watched the Gunsmith—the "hero" of his forthcoming opus on the Great American West—lift his glass to his lips, his eyes firmly on the lean cowpuncher, and take a drink.

"I don't think you're the Gunsmith at all, mister! I think you're a fake."

"That's right," said Clint. "I'm not the Gunsmith. My name is Clint Adams."

"Mister, you're full of shit."

"Jesse, don't . . ." one of his companions said.

But he was too late—Jesse had already gone for his gun. Abner Frolicher, with a fresh cigar in his mouth, just waiting to be lighted, very nearly chewed the whole end off as his bugging eyes took in the scene before him. He asked himself later—and kept asking himself in the days to come—whether he could believe what he saw.

He watched the cowboy's hand strike like a snake to his six-gun, while Clint Adams still held his beer in his gunhand. Within the next second—or even less, Abner later wrote—Jesse had cleared his gun from its holster. The Gunsmith's glass of beer fell to the floor, but before it hit, Clint had his Colt out and up, and a single shot had sent Jesse's gun flying across the barroom, while a scream of pain, rage, and astonishment was torn from the cowboy's mouth.

Instant silence claimed the saloon. Not even breathing could be heard as the would-be gunman from the Double Bar B bent in pain toward his gunhand. Not even a gasp or whimper escaped him; perhaps his astonishment was greater than his pain.

"Jesus," murmured Abner Frolicher. "Jesus, the man drew and shot him *after* the man's gun had cleared leather!" But no one heard him, and later, recalling it, Abner wondered if he had even said the words aloud.

"My apologies, Mr. Harrigan, but I did try to avoid a fight. And, for the matter of that, maybe I have." Clint smiled then at the group of four. "If Mr. Harrigan there has no objections, maybe he'll let me buy you boys a drink and we'll forget this little matter, though you, you better go see Doc Joyner for some linament on that hand."

Quietly, Clint put money on the bar, and with a nod to Zeke Wools, turned and walked out of the room without a backward look.

But Abner Frolicher, quivering with excitement, did not fail to notice that as the Gunsmith walked away from the bar with his back to the four cowboys, he kept his eyes firmly on himself seated against the wall at the back of the room—obviously for any sign of suspicious activity.

Thus, Abner felt himself a part of the Gunsmith's

life—at least a part of his activity, for a moment—and it gave him something. That is, he felt differently about himself from that moment when the Gunsmith had watched him for verification of what might be going on behind his back. It was a terrific moment in the life of Abner Frolicher.

Clint took certain precautions when he went to bed that night. Carefully, he locked the window and the door, wedging the back of the room's only chair under the knob for good measure. Then he lay down on the bed fully clothed.

He slept with his gun under his pillow, for extra safety, and also slept lightly. And so when he heard the steps coming down the corridor outside he wasn't surprised and in fact was out of bed, with his gun in his hand as the knock came at the door.

"Who is it?"

"Jacqueline."

"Are you alone?"

"Of course. Oh, please let me in."

He was at the side of the door, his gun drawn, and now with his free hand he turned the key and took the chair away.

"Come in."

She was already through the door, and he closed it behind her.

"What's happened?" he asked, going to the lamp on the table and lighting it.

"Please excuse my appearance, but—but I was frightened, and you'd said I might call on you for help."

"Sit down," he said. "On the edge of the bed there. Take your time."

She was almost out of breath, her face was flushed, a couple of strands of hair were coming down. She was evidently in her nightdress but all was well covered with her voluminous traveling cloak.

"Maybe you heard them," she said. "No, I guess you didn't. At my window."

"Heard who? You're around the corner from me, so you're facing the alley."

"Of course. You couldn't have heard. They were calling up, calling me—names. And Todd. My window was open. I always like to sleep with the fresh air. And in fact, I had gone to sleep early because I was very tired. I'd visited the cemetery this afternoon—yesterday, I guess, actually—to see Todd. . . ." She bowed her head and he knew she was fighting her tears.

"Who were they?" he asked, placing the chair under the knob again.

"I don't know. Some men. Three maybe, four. I don't know. They sounded like maybe they'd been drinking. They—they were horrible! I can't tell you how it was. Oh, I'm so sorry to disturb you this way, I just—well, it upset me. I'm sorry. After seeing Todd's grave, I—I guess I'm a weak person. Not one of your frontier types at all."

"I think you're doing just fine," Clint said, finding it difficult to take his eyes off her.

"It isn't just this, what happened now at my window. I went out to the cemetery and I could feel some of the people on my way, how their hate was coming at me."

"Well, they apparently loved old Crosby and since they figure he was done in by your husband, I suppose . . ."

"But they didn't even give Todd a trial."

And suddenly she leaned forward, covering her face with her hands, and began to sob. He had seated himself on the bed beside her, with some distance between them, but now he moved closer and slipped his arm around her bowed shoulders and felt her wracking sobs against his chest.

Gradually her crying died down and stopped and she drew back, dabbing at her eyes with a small handkerchief.

"I—I'm sorry. I lost control of myself. Please excuse me."

"It's good for you to get it out. Let it all out. You've been holding it in too long."

"I'm sorry. . . ."

Her cloak had fallen open and he not only had a view of a part of her leg, but a delicious glance at part of a superbly shaped breast. Clint felt his breath catch and an immediate stirring in his crotch. But she was swiftly aware of the situation and pulled the cloak together.

"My—I *am* sorry. . . ."

"I am not," Clint said with a quiet grin. "It was my great pleasure. However, all from the point of view of admiring a work of art." And he bowed his head in mock humility and she laughed unexpectedly.

Her eyes, a moment ago filled with tears, were now almost dancing with good humor at his friendly caper.

"I must get back to my room," she said.

"I'll see you back."

She seemed about to protest, but he was already on

his feet, opening the door, and in a moment they were at her room.

"I am not trying to invade your privacy," he said. "But I do insist on looking at your room to see that you are safe here. If those men have been drinking, they may get some more into them and there could be trouble."

"Thank you," she said and he followed her in.

The room was a replica of his own, except that the window looked out onto the alley alongside the hotel, while his overlooked Main Street. He checked the window latch, the lock on the door, and cautioned her to place the chair back under the knob, showing her how.

"Thank you," she said again when he told her that should she hear the slightest strange noise, or any sort of disturbance, she should call him immediately.

"I will."

"Promise?"

She nodded. "I will . . . I will . . ."

He turned and started toward the doorway.

"Clint . . ."

He turned as she came toward him and stood there and reached out and took his hand in hers.

She didn't say anything, and neither did he. But it was not necessary to say a thing. He turned again and walked out of the room. In his own bed again he fell asleep immediately, with a quiet smile on his face, and in his body.

When he awakened dawn was just touching the windowsill, the sun not yet risen. Instantly, he heard the light tapping on his bedroom door and sat up on the edge of the bed with his feet on the floor. His heart beat rapidly, wondering whether it was Jackie changing her mind. He knew how a great sorrow can sometimes call forth a great passion.

He stood, holding his six-gun, though he knew it was liable not to be an enemy, not in the daytime at any rate.

The knock came again. He stepped forward and opened the door, again moving swiftly to one side—just in case.

"I've got a message for you," the girl said. "From Sophie." He saw immediately that it was Angie, the blonde who had first greeted him in Sunshine Wells so amiably, whom he'd met at the Screaming Eagle; and he realized that there was a connection between Sophie O'Govern's operation and Boyd Harrigan's. Both run by Torb Mill?

"Come in," he said.

He locked the door behind her, admiring the way she walked all the way into the room.

"Had the night off at the Eagle," she said, "and when I was visiting a friend at Sophie's, she sent me to tell you to keep a close watch on your friend. Sophie said you'd know who she meant."

"Gotcha," Clint said, and he reached behind him and locked the door.

"I see you were expectin' me," she said.

"But of course."

He was standing close to her now and could smell the strong perfume she was wearing. He didn't mind it. Indeed, it seemed to add to the animal quality of her appeal. Her blatant innocence. And the slight flush in her cheeks now suddenly appearing added something to the picture that brought the word ''virginity'' to his mind. Strange, but there it was. He knew she must have had a lot of men, and yet there was this air of innocence— yes, virginity. There was for sure something virginal in the girl, that is, as he saw it, something fresh and as yet untrammelled; something that the army of men who had marched between her legs had failed to spoil. He was touched as he had seldom been touched. And he wondered if it might be as a result of his encounter the night before with Jackie Gandy. Though it didn't matter. What mattered now was that he was rigidly ready for her as she finally removed the last of her clothing.

He, meanwhile had dropped his trousers, removed his shirt, and stepped toward her, totally naked, thrusting his hard penis right between her legs and up into her ready vagina.

He slipped his hands under her buttocks as she hooked her arms around his neck, her legs around his waist, and as he marched her to the bed she was already riding his great penis, gasping against his face and into his ear.

Then he had her down on her back on the bed and was ploughing long, slow strokes into her wetness. And in the next moment they were both awash with their mixed juices as they subsided into each other's arms and legs and lips and hands in the most utter joy.

FIVE

Torb Mill struck the wooden match on his thumbnail and waited a second or two for the flame to settle before holding it to his companion's cigar.

"Got it?" he asked, smiling in the corners of his narrow eyes.

"Mmm," his companion murmured with pleasure, blowing out a soft light cloud of fragrant Havana tobacco.

"I have some—uh—papers here for you to sign." And he turned toward his desk.

"Darling, can't we attend to that later? I'm enjoying my cigar."

Torb Mill pursed his lips, put down the papers he had just picked up, and turned back to the woman who was seated in the easy chair.

"Lilly, my dear, of course." And now he was smiling amiably as he admired her firm figure filling the riding habit that followed every curve, moved even with her easy breathing, and which had been exciting his passion ever since the moment she had walked into his office.

"I'd thought we might just get the business thing out of the way," he said in an explanatory tone.

She was looking up at him as he stood over her. "I'd like a drink, Torb. Some of that marvelous brandy you brought back with you."

"From Frisco?"

"That's the stuff."

He had walked to a cabinet at the side of the room and was already opening a bottle which had been standing next to two glasses.

Pouring, he said, "We'll drink to our new enterprise."

"Which is?"

He handed her a glass and then raised his own. "Us."

She put her cigar down then, laying it carefully in the ashtray on the little table beside the armchair. She was a woman in her early thirties, considered by anyone who had met her to be beautiful.

Torb was standing close to her, looking down at her bosom, which he could see was absolutely straining at the stitches of her orange silk riding blouse. Her dark hair was spilling over her collar, in a loose coiffure, and her high forehead shone from the late afternoon sunlight that was sparkling through the large window behind the desk.

"Here's to us," he said, raising his glass.

Her English heritage shone through her speech now as she said, "Quite!"

"Quite!" he repeated after her with a laugh. "You sound like a duchess!"

"Are you objecting?"

"Not at all. I find your accent as exciting as some—
uh—other things."

"Like what, Mr. Mill?"

"Like, your eyes."

"I have two of them, isn't that nice."

"And you have two arms."

"And hands."

"And two legs," he said, feeling his blood race.

"Twos are nice."

"And especially these two," he said, reaching down
and fondling her breasts. "I'm crazy about you, Lil,"
he said.

"I wouldn't expect otherwise, my dear. I'm crazy
about you."

"Shall we drink to that?"

"To what?" She was almost off the chair now and
on the floor as his hands continued to fondle her, finally
reaching inside her clothing to cup her springy breasts
with their large, hard nipples.

"To love," he said, as she pulled his bone-hard
organ out of his trousers and buried it in her eager
mouth.

"Oh God, Torb—fuck me. Fuck me!"

It was pitch dark in the room when they finally came
together to release their pent-up passion in a thrashing
explosion on the bear rug in front of his desk.

They lay there now, gasping for air, sweating a good
bit, still entwined.

"My God," Lilly said after a while. "Is the door
locked?"

"I locked it. I hope you don't think I'd make that
mistake again."

"Dear God, no. Once was enough."

He grinned against her ear in the dark. "Remember that once was the 'once' that changed our lives."

She nestled to him then and his erection returned, mightier than before.

"My God," she whispered. "I need it so."

"You've got it, my dear."

And this time he rode her fast and hard while her cries broke softly into the black room.

Much later, they awakened after sleeping together on the floor.

The knocking was loud and insistent.

Torb was up on his feet quickly, anger striking through him as the pounding continued. Pulling on his clothes quickly, while Lilly picked up hers and hurried into another room and out of sight, he suddenly remembered that he'd made an appointment with Harry Bones and the town council to discuss some important matters. Only why was the knocking so insistent, so loud? What the hell was the matter?

It was Bert Smiles at the door.

"What the hell is all the racket about!" demanded Mill.

"It's trouble, Mr. Mill. Jesse Ollinger and some of his buddies from the Double Bar B shot up the Screaming Eagle trying to get even with Boyd Harrigan on account of the way he sided with that Gunsmith feller."

"So why do you come out here to bother me with it?" demanded the furious Torb Mill. "You think that's something special! Tell it to Bones! That's the marshal's business."

"Harry is shot up, too," Bert said. "That's what I got to tell you."

The news hit him right in the chest and he almost took a step backward. Then, in fact, he did step backward to admit the deputy into the room.

"What happened?" he demanded, as soon as they were in the office with the door shut. "Tell me!"

"Jesse and his buddies, they come into the Eagle and started jawin' with Zeke and some of the men there, and in walks Boyd and they lit into him, telling him what a shithead he was letting that Gunsmith feller get away with backwaterin' Jesse, and takin' unfair advantage of him and like that."

"Was Adams there?"

"Adams?" Bert Smiles looked stupidly at his questioner.

"That's his name, you fool. Was he there?"

"No. He wasn't there. But Boyd, he tried to cool things down and next thing Jesse went for his hogleg and by God he outdrew Boyd and shot him."

"How bad?"

"Not good. Boyd's at Joyner's."

"Where's Jesse?"

"Took off. Could be out at the Double Bar."

Torb Mill was already reaching for his hat.

At the door he paused, so suddenly that the deputy almost ran into him.

"And Bones?" he said. "How did he get in on it?"

"Harry come in and the four of them went at him."

"What do you mean—went at him?"

"They beat the shit out of him. Pistol-whipped him, by God! And they shot him, too, in the leg."

"They kill him? Goddammit, Smiles. Give me the straight of it!"

"Naw. No, they beat him. God, it was awful! Blood all over the place."

"That the whole of it?"

Bert Smiles nodded, and said, "The whole of it, so help me."

Torb turned back to the door, but stopped again, and turned to face the deputy. "And what about you? Where were you, Deputy Smiles, when your marshal of Sunshine Wells was getting himself near killed?" Torb Mill stood there hard as a singletree in front of the other man, who had started to sweat at his cutting words.

Bert Smiles's lip started to tremble, one eye twitched, he lifted his hands, almost bringing them together in front of his chest, and held them there—together. And he said nothing. Not a thing.

Torb Mill opened the door.

"Get out," he said.

"In a town like this someone like yourself sticks out like a diamond stickpin in a saddle bum's bandanna," Clint was saying to Jacqueline. "And so . . ."

"And so, you're saying that Todd would be easily noticed, too."

"Right." He nodded. "I am saying that anybody'd remember him, especially if he took off right after killing the town's most famous citizen."

"Of course." They were in a side street, on their way toward the town cemetery.

"Take the town marshal, Harry Bones," Clint continued. "For sure if there'd been a stranger in town he'd have spotted him, and then if he'd suddenly been missing, he'd wonder what had happened."

"But what has that to—"

"It has this to do with it, that it couldn't have been a stranger who killed Crosby. It had to be a local person."

"I see. I see, maybe it was someone with a grudge or something against the old man."

"Maybe that, maybe something else that we don't quite see right now," Clint answered. "It seems Crosby was always ready to give a loan, from what I hear about town. He didn't give handouts, he gave loans."

"And loans have to be paid off," she said.

"With interest. Maybe even with other strings attached," Clint added.

"Of course."

"Some people who borrow simply pay off their debt, like at certain time periods, something like that, as best they can," Clint went on. "But then there are some who get to complaining about having to pay the extra, the interest on it."

"I can see how that could become hateful."

"And a man could even get to hating the man he'd borrowed from," Clint put in.

"Yes, yes. You're saying that a man might find that motive enough to kill?"

"What do you think?"

"I don't know. Oh, I don't know. I only know it couldn't have been—no, not couldn't have been—it *wasn't* Todd."

They were silent now as they approached the cemetery, a plot of land outside the town, with nothing special to mark it except the large, raw stone that stood in a plot in the center of other, much smaller stones and markers.

"That has got to be Crosby's," the Gunsmith said to the woman who had fallen abruptly silent.

But Jacqueline Gandy wasn't listening. Her eyes were on the mound of earth a distance away from the other graves; it was a grave with no stone, no marker to indicate who it was. She had found it the other day.

Clint stood still, following her with his eyes as she walked slowly to the grave and stood there looking down with her hands clasped together at her waist.

He watched her kneel down and reach out to touch the mound of earth, as though to assure herself that it was really there.

He waited, turning away now to allow her privacy, and walked over to the huge rock that dominated the cemetery. It was a jagged piece of stone and must have required an extra strong stone bolt to bring it to the cemetery. Jagged, hard, dark in color—he wondered how much the stone reflected the character of the man lying below it.

Looking up then, he saw a man walking toward him. It was Fabio Joyner and he was carrying a small bunch of flowers.

Clint had walked back toward the doctor, leaving Jacqueline Gandy at graveside, and now he nodded a greeting as Joyner drew up beside him.

"I've come on behalf of one of my patients," the doctor said, as he showed the bunch of flowers. "You see me in a unique role. But what can a man do—A, when he is a member of the medical profession, and B, when he is a fool for feeling." And a sly grin turned his grave countenance into something rather joyful.

Clint Adams was glad to see him. "I only just heard about the action in the Screaming Eagle, that the marshal got it kind of badly."

"He'll mend. He is a tough old boy." He waved the flowers again. "These are for Millicent. His wife. It's—well, I hope it's all right for me to say. Their anniversary. And he has to stay in bed at least another day or two. So, well, here I be." His grin had become a smile. Warm. "I don't know how to say this, Adams, but I'm glad you're here. There is something dark in this town, as you can well see and feel."

"You have hopes that I will dispel it?"

"No. I have hopes that this event with Crosby, and the presence of Gandy's widow, and surely yourself, will lead our wretched community to see its need to mend."

"You know, Doc, I've been feeling that underneath a lot of this feeling in town that Ephraim Crosby was such a great fellow, that there's also a feeling that he wasn't all that terrific. I mean. I don't get the sense of a town sunk into mourning exactly."

"I know just what you mean," Joyner said, with a brisk nod of his head. "I see it, too, and I've been here longer than you. But it isn't said, it isn't out loud. I think there are some people in town who might side with your thinking that Gandy got a real raw deal."

Without either of the two men saying anything about it, they started walking toward Gandy's grave—the mound of earth that supported no stone or wooden marker.

As they approached, Jacqueline looked up, and both Clint and Joyner were struck by the devastated look in her eyes. It was clear to Clint that at this particular moment she had no understanding of the horrendous thing that had happened; and hardly any understanding that her husband was indeed really dead.

Clint's impulse was to go to her and comfort her, but he resisted it. He knew full well his feelings were not completely platonic. In fact, he found the woman by the graveside absolutely desirable. And, strangely, he had the feeling, too, that she liked him, maybe even wanted him, yet was not herself aware of it.

Doc Joyner held up the scraggly bunch of flowers that he had picked for Harry Bones to put on his wife's grave.

"Got these for the marshal's wife," he said. "But I see you don't have any flowers. I'd like to offer you one or two of these."

Clint thought she was going to break right then and there, and he knew that Joyner regretted what he'd said. But she controlled herself, her lip trembling just a little. Clint thought she controlled herself magnificently.

"How kind of you," she said, her voice very close to a whisper. "How very . . ." He couldn't hear the rest as Joyner drew two flowers from the slender bunch and handed them to her.

Both men removed their hats now and waited while Jacqueline placed the flowers carefully on the innocuous gravesite. They left her then and walked over to place the rest at the small wooden marker where Millicent Bones lay.

"Harry asked me to say a few words if I'd a mind to," Doc said.

"Good enough," Clint said.

When they were through Joyner said, "I never know what to say at such a time."

"You did fine," Clint said.

"Millie was a nice lady. Real nice."

"And Harry?"

They had stopped to wait for Jacqueline.

"Harry?" The doctor pursed his lips, reached in his pocket for his pipe, and loaded it, his eyes vague with thought. "Harry Bones is a mystery," he said.

"What do you mean?" Clint asked.

"Harry just up and appeared one day. 'Least it seemed that way. Came from nowhere. Met Millicent and married her. I'd reckon ten years ago it was."

"How did he get the marshal's job?"

"Nobody else wanted it. When Tim Witherspoon took an overdose of lead the job was open."

Clint didn't say anything more, for Jackie Gandy had joined them and the three of them walked back to town in the late afternoon sunlight that came slanting across the prairie, and entered the town without the slightest disturbance to man or beast.

The day broke gently over the plain and the distant caps of the Absorokas sparkled white under the azure sky. Those mountains held the snow all summer long, but Clint Adams long knew how dry the air was in those jagged peaks. A man could stay outdoors in his shirt, and even just his long-handles without a shiver if need be, the air was that clean—not a drop of moisture in it.

But he and Duke were on the plain now, taking the south trail out of town, long before the town was up and about. He walked the big black gelding for a good distance, enjoying the morning as behind him he heard a dog barking, a cock crowing.

"We'll just amble it a bit, Duke boy," Clint said. He often talked to the big black, who was more friend than horse.

Duke's big head bobbed as he shook off a couple of flies, and Clint knew he wanted to run, but he held him. He wanted to think, he wanted to get his notions about the Gandy killing in order. Right now there were a lot of loose ends and questions.

Why had Todd Gandy been set up for the killing of Ephraim Crosby? Why had the deputy, Bert Smiles, rigged, or helped rig, Gandy's "escape"? Who was Smiles working for? Surely not himself; the man wasn't that bright. What did the town really think about Crosby? Who was his widow? He'd have to look her up. And who was Torb Mill?

Clint felt the presence of both Torb Mill and Lilly Crosby heavily on the whole scene. And then there were the Double Bar B hands. They seemed more gunmen than cowhands. And who were they working for?

And then suddenly, as he was fording a creek about the middle of the hot forenoon, he remembered the Indians who had attacked the stagecoach. Why had they come to mind just now, he wondered as he sat Duke while the big horse drank from the creek and cooled his legs.

He remembered now that the little band attacking the stage had been drunk, and this brought to mind remarks he'd caught in town about the reservation Indians getting hold of whiskey. Someone had been selling the redmen whiskey, which was against the law, not to mention dangerous.

He crossed the creek and rode through a stand of cottonwoods and box elders, and in the distance he saw a string of smoke rising above a screen of trees, behind which was a high butte. He drew rein and pulled out his field glasses for a closer look. It gave him a funny feeling to discover that he was looking at an Indian camp, and he realized he must be near the Shoshone reservation. But he wasn't sure now whether the men who had chased the stage were Shoshone or from another tribe. They had been drunk as skunks.

He was on the point of lowering his field glasses and slipping them back into their case when something caught his eye. Something moving just inside the line of trees. He moved the glasses away so that he was looking at something else, then returned them to where he had been looking.

At that moment, a horse and rider appeared. It was obviously a white man. Following him was a shallow box wagon pulled by a pair of white horses, with two men in the seat.

The rider looked back at the wagon and waved them on, and then rode toward an opening in another stand of trees that seemed to line a narrow creek. Clint set his eyes on the wagon now, trying to see what was in the box. But he could tell nothing. A tarp covered whatever it was the men were hauling toward the smoke that was becoming more vague in the hot noonday sky.

The marshal of Sunshine Wells lay in the bed with his body throbbing. It seemed to hurt all over. But it was pleasant watching the young woman moving about the room. She moved easily, her movements were simple, clean—just like her glance and the way she spoke to him. And though Harry Bones was not an especially vain man he did like the way she called him "Marshal" and "Marshal Bones." This was Doc Joyner's daughter Kerry, who helped him out with patients who needed that something extra. Well, Harry thought, Joyner by God had done something else good besides being a medic.

"What can I get you, Marshal?" She smiled fondly down at him. She was a girl of twenty-some, with long cornsilk hair, blue eyes, and a spring in her step that showed a joy for life that delighted the young men around town—and the old ones too, for that matter. While her calico dress did not a thing to hide her full bosom from the lascivious looks of a number of young and older men—and the honed tongues of nattering women—Kerry was a modest girl; she didn't flirt, and as her father put it, she didn't let anyone "get previous with her." It was the life in her that bothered some people. Her sparkle. Her happiness.

Harry Bones thought she was lovely. She reminded him of Millicent, though a good bit younger. And she reminded him of his own youth, which—he surmised—

might be the reason why certain tongues and pointing fingers in the town disapproved of her; for surely she reminded other men, too.

"You can get me a new body," he said in answer to her question about what she could get him. He thought she had the clearest eyes he'd seen in good while.

She gave a little laugh. "And what about your old body?" she asked. "You don't want to throw it away after it has served you all your life, now do you?"

"You got me there, miss," he said.

She reached down and arranged his bed covers and then looked around the room to see if there was anything else that needed her attention.

It was Harry's room, in his house, which he had shared with Millicent. They'd had no children and now, even in his physical pain from the beating he'd received from the men in the Screaming Eagle, he could wish that he had a daughter like Kerry Joyner.

When she went out of the room he tested himself again, as he had been doing every so often since he'd been brought home and put in bed. His side hurt, so did his leg, the one with the old wound from the fight with the Shoshone up on Skinhead Creek, and his gun arm was sore; not to forget the left side of his face and head where some sweetheart had laid a gun barrel none too gently.

But he was glad to be alive. In fact, he felt better than he'd felt in a long time: since Millicent had died. He felt more alive, even though battered and bruised, with maybe a cracked rib or two, a swollen left hand, but nothing broken, nothing some rest couldn't handle.

He was already thinking of what he was going to do
when he got up and about.

Kerry came in again. "You've got a visitor," she
said. "Do you want to see anyone?"

"Who is it?"

But before the girl could answer the voice came
through the half open door.

"It's me." And the tall figure of Torb Mill strode
into the room, almost pushing past the girl who managed to step aside in time.

"Excuse me, miss, but I'm in a hurry," Mill said.

Harry Bones watched the flush rise and fall in the
girl's cheeks.

"I need to talk to you, Harry?"

The marshal of Sunshine Wells had managed to push
himself up onto his elbows so that he could look more
or less evenly at his visitor. Anger had darkened his
face, but Torb Mill didn't appear to notice.

"You'll excuse us, young lady," Torb said, without
looking at the girl.

"And you will apologize to Miss Joyner right now,
Mill," snapped the man in the bed. "And I mean right
now!"

Now Mill saw through his own importance and realized his mistake. Marshal Harry Bones might be old, he
might no longer be the fast gun of former times, and he
might be badly laid up, but he was still piss and vine-
gar. And Torb Mill cursed himself for having forgotten,
and so had put himself in the position of being
backwatered. But he had common sense, too, and saw
what was needed.

"I apologize, Miss Joyner. I have been rude, impatient, inconsiderate. It is that there has been so much trouble in town without our marshal up and about, and, too, talk of possible Indian trouble, that I let it get to me. I do apologize.'' And he beamed. His smile was one of his best weapons. It didn't settle either of the other two people in the room, but both accepted the apology.

Kerry said nothing. To Harry Bones's delight, she simply gave a brief nod and left the room. He wanted to laugh. By God, that girl was something. By God, if he was ten, fifteen years younger . . .

''Take that chair there,'' he said, and he was not smiling. ''And let's hear it. I'll more'n likely be up and about come tomorrer.''

Torb Mill drew the chair closer to the bed and looked into the watery eyes of Harry Bones. And he saw that something was different. All the same he had his plan. And he needed Bones. What was more, Bones might try getting uppity—like just now—and he might let him get away with it, but in the final count, Harry would do exactly as he was told. He would have to.

SIX

Now it was evening, and as the cool entered the dying day, Clint Adams rode into sight of the town. A few lights had started to dot the streets, maybe four or five—he didn't count them—but he had the sudden feeling of an inexplicable loneliness that seemed to pervade Sunshine Wells. In a word, it was an unhappy place. He was struck by this summation as he rode toward the dark little town set against the darkening sky. And his eyes turned to the evening star. Somehow he felt better seeing that shining permanence in the great sky.

As he and Duke closed in on the town his thoughts returned to the abandoned team and wagon he had come upon in the stand of cottonwoods and box elders. Whatever had been underneath the tarpaulin had been taken away. There were unshod pony tracks and the prints of white men and the shod hooves of their horses. Obviously the wagon and its accompanying team of men had been met by two mounted Indians. It had evidently been a peaceful meeting. Only the men and their cargo were nowhere in sight. Nor was there any sign—at least at first look—as to what their cargo had been. But as he had stood there in the heat of the mid-afternoon, the Gunsmith became aware of the odor of something that was unmistakable. Whiskey.

Suddenly he had felt them near, and in a moment he had retreated, leading Duke, through the trees. And from a thick clump of bullberry bushes he watched the three men returning to the wagon. The first two men he had never seen before. But the third, bringing up the rear, was one whose acquaintance he had most recently—and violently—made. It was Deputy Bert Smiles.

Clint was well hidden by the bullberry bush, and he could hear them. Nothing special. The only mystery was why they had delivered whiskey to the Shoshone. For what purpose? He had discovered it was not a large tribe, but a small band. He had the clear feeling that no money had been involved. And indeed, the Indians didn't trade in money. Clearly, the payment or barter had included some value that was quite other than the usual. When they were well on their way, he mounted Duke, and with deep foreboding had pointed the big black gelding toward Sunshine Wells.

Now, approaching the lip of the gray little town, he realized that the killing of Ephraim Crosby and railroading of Todd Gandy were elements of something on a larger scale; something—and he could only hazard the guess—that could possibly involve the military peace between the Indians and the white men.

It was Kerry Joyner who opened the door to Clint almost immediately following his knock. And at the surprised look on his face, the girl started to laugh, blushed, and finally couldn't control herself and let herself burst into a wide sunshine smile.

"You must be Mr. Adams," she said. "I'll just bet you are. I've heard all about you."

"All?" said Clint, delighted by this new and unexpected presence in his life.

"The marshal is feeling better, and I am sure he'll be glad to see you." And then a sudden thought swept into her face. "Or—I don't know. You know, he isn't always so glad to see just anybody."

Clint was charmed at the way she was treating him. There was nothing at all false in her pleasure. And in her next sentence it became clear to him why she was speaking the way she was.

"My dad thinks a lot of you, and he's been telling me all about you. I mean," she added, "all that he knows."

"Maybe he doesn't know me all that well," Clint said, following her into the small house where they were met by Steve, the grim, baleful, gray cat who walked over to the visitor and, to Clint's astonishment, rubbed against his leg.

"I see you have a way with cats," the girl said, as they crossed the room.

"Fact is, I'm irresistible," the Gunsmith said. "Uh—to cats," he added. Then he said, "We already met at the office."

But she had already called through the open door to the figure sitting up in bed. "Are you ready for a visitor?"

"Send him in. I already heerd his voice."

Kerry Joyner's figure—from the rear, the side, the front—had absolutely captivated Clint, and he almost missed his cue, standing there with a lively erection struggling at his trouser leg.

Then she was gone.

"Come in, Adams. Don't stand there pickin' yer nose," the crusty man of the law said, as Steve streaked under the bed. "What kin I do for you?"

"First I wanted to see how you were doing." Clint had regained his composure with the disappearance of the girl, and took a chair at the side of the bed.

"I am alive. Can't ask much more'n that, I reckon." He reached to his pajama pocket and took out the makings and began building a smoke. His callused fingers were swift, deft at this small but important craft.

Then Clint told him about what he had seen near the Shoshone village: the wagon, the smell of whiskey, the men.

The marshal struck a lucifer and lighted his cigarette. "Figgers." The word came out with a finality that told Clint the marshal had known all along about Bert Smiles.

"You can use it however you will," Clint said. "But if you want my advice—and more than likely you don't—I'd act fast."

"Act fast—huh?" The tight, nut-colored face above the drooping brown mustache turned fully on his visitor as the lawman sniffed, swallowed some phlegm, and scratched at his Adam's apple, all without removing the cigarette from the corner of his mouth.

"I am saying that there was something in their way that read they were damn sure of themselves and could be about to do something, or that something was about ready to happen."

Harry Bones nodded then, a glint in his eyes. "Gotcha. I see what you're gettin' to. And I 'preciate it, Adams. You're a man—I can tell—who sees what's in front of him. Most don't."

Clint took a cigar from his shirt pocket. "Mind if I fire this thing?"

"I mind nothing but my own business," Harry Bones said crisply. "My business bein' the law mostly, I guess. And I am now asking you to sign on as deputy."

"Since I guess you need a new one? Thanks, but I have already tried that once, and I've sworn off it."

"Sworn off it?" The eyes cut to him like an eagle's.

"I have my gunsmithy to handle."

"Adams, you can't drop your gun. You might say you're Clint Adams, but to one helluva lot of people you're the Gunsmith. And you know that in the business, there's only one way a man retires. Hickok learned that."

"I know," Clint said with a nod. He knew very well the burden his old friend Wild Bill had carried. "But I'm still a dealer in my trade—repairing, rebuilding, remodeling guns."

"I am sorry to hear that."

"It doesn't mean I won't help you if I can," Clint said.

A sort of grin stole into the marshal's eyes then. "Gotcha," he said. "Good enough."

They settled down then and dropped the parrying that had been woven into their conversation.

Clint took a drag on his Havana and blew a cloud of smoke toward the ceiling. "You're dropping Bert?"

"Nope. He's more use to me where I can keep a eye on him."

"Do you figure the Shoshone are building up to an uprising, or is it just some renegades who want to let off steam? I mean, is there a plan—someone behind the whiskey thing?"

"I ain't sure." Harry Bones shifted his weight, then with a sigh lay back on his pillow.

At this point Kerry Joyner came in with two steaming mugs of coffee, and Clint Adams's eyes swept to her buttocks as she bent toward the man in the bed.

When she left Bones said, "I can't see Runs-His-Horses in on anything like that. He's a tough old boy; sure don't care for the whites, but he don't allow the whiskey in his camp, I know for a fact."

"Then how come the wagon?"

"You know how some of them young bucks get feisty. They ain't allowed to go hunt, or do much of anything exceptin' set around camp."

"I know," Clint nodded. "I've seen it. They don't have any way to let off steam, like in the old days."

"So there's always some who's dissatisfied and jumpy, lookin' for excitement."

"So you're suggesting it's maybe them that Bert and his buddies are dealing with," Clint said.

The marshal nodded. " 'Course, it could be more'n just Bert. But the thing is, Runs-His-Horses is no blanket chief. He's one of the old-timers, a tough old boy. But he wants peace. I know that for a fact."

"I've been thinking the same thing—that maybe it's more than Bert. But who?"

"I dunno."

But Clint saw doubt in the marshal's eyes, heard it in his tone.

"Would this have anything to do with Crosby's killing?" Clint asked.

"Jesus! How d'you figure something like that?"

"I am just asking," Clint said calmly. "You've got two things happening in a town where nothing ever happens." He spread his hands apart, palms up, and looked directly at Harry Bones. "Maybe—maybe not. But let's take a look at it."

"You're suggesting that Gandy did not kill Crosby."

"I'm not suggesting, I am saying. I really doubt he had anything to do with it; I do believe he was set up."

"You're saying that Gandy didn't kill Crosby, or that he had anything to do with this whiskey situation, either?"

"That part I don't know—about the whiskey. Although, from what I hear of the man—of course, through his wife—I have to doubt he did. Hell, I can't see a man like Todd Gandy having anything to do with a Bert Smiles."

"Money is money," the marshal of Sunshine Wells said grimly.

"There's something we have to take a careful look at, is all I'm saying," Clint insisted. "Something here bigger than Ephraim Crosby's murder and bigger than Bert Smiles and his buddies selling whiskey to some renegade Shoshone."

"But why do you claim they're connected? Shit, you can't connect a stonebolt and a church service."

"I don't know why. I just have a feeling—a feeling that there is something." He took a long look at the marshal then. "And I want to tell you I have got a real strong feeling that you smell a rat, too."

"Maybe. Maybe I do, I dunno," the marshal said warily.

Clint leaned forward in his chair now. "Look," he said, "this whole thing smells. It's too pat, and it's got too many holes in it. Somebody's shoved the idea through that Gandy killed Crosby and nobody's questioned it."

"Maybe," Harry Bones said carefully.

"But you must have thought it over by now. I mean, time has passed. Can't you recollect any Sunshine Wells man with a grudge against Crosby? It could have been an old grudge that needed to be scored. Or could be someone just hated him."

He studied the marshal for a moment while silence claimed them both.

Then Clint resumed. "Tell me: How did you feel about Crosby? Did you shine his boots like everybody else in town? Let's have the straight of it."

Harry Bones sighed, shifted his weight again, somewhat painfully, and reached for his pipe and tobacco.

"I got to admit that as far as personal goes I didn't cotton to old Ephraim so much. I never felt he earned all the big how-de-do stuff that went on. 'Ceptin', I never said any of this to anybody in town. You keep it to yourself, Adams. Hell, I need this job. Since—since my wife up and died I—I got to keep going somehow.

She is buried here, and I don't want to leave Sunshine. So I keep my mouth shut, exceptin' of course where the law is concerned."

"This that we're talking about concerns the law," Clint said evenly.

"Can't say as how I blame you for augurin' on it," Harry Bones said, using the old-fashioned word carefully. "How did I see old Ephraim?" He struck the wooden match on his thumbnail and then, tamping the tobacco in his pipe with his thick middle finger, drew on the flame, releasing a large pillow of smoke into the room.

"He was a miser. Greedy. Short-tempered. Hard as a silver dollar. I always figgered he liked folks kowtowin' to him; people beholden for their homes or jobs or whatever. I never took nothing from him. I was careful not to." His eyes swept the room. "It's why me and Millicent lived small. But it was all ours. I am a man who likes his independence. I will tell you that, Adams."

"But wasn't he kind of jolly now and again? Didn't he like a good laugh, a good story?"

A sour look came over the marshal's face. "I never knew him like that. He drank heavily and he had the gout. He wasn't often in a happy mood; let me put it like that."

"How old was he? Got any idea?"

"I dunno. Hell, I do believe I heard he was in his late sixties, something like that."

"I heard he was a strong man, though, in good health, nimble, handy with tools." Clint fed the words to the marshal, watching closely how the lawman reacted. "I heard he was full of zip, and in fact, hot for the girls."

"No!" Harry Bones made a throwaway gesture with his hand. "Hell, he had trouble walking; not only had gout, but some years back got throwed by his hoss and busted his leg bad. Limped. Had to have a cane. There was nothing spry about Crosby."

"What time was he found?"

"Late. A good bit after midnight."

"Can you tell me how he was dressed? I mean, wasn't long after midnight, long after an old man's bedtime?"

"You'd think so—yup," allowed Harry Bones. "He was dressed normal. He had his pants, his shirt, and coat, boots."

"Hat?"

"Come to think of it, he didn't have his hat."

"How about his walking stick?"

"Cane? By golly, I don't remember seein' it."

"No cane, and he had a game leg. No hat—outdoors in the middle of the night. That could be. But—no cane!"

"I don't recollect seein' it; and in fact, I did ask about it later. Somebody—I don't remember who—said it was taken to his house."

"And somebody told me he was found a good distance from his home," Clint went on. "And late at night. It smells, Bones, it smells."

"I don't disagree with you," Harry Bones said. "I did wonder about the cane, and what the old boy was doing that far from his house in the dead of night. But nothing came to me."

"Nothing comes to me either," Clint said, and then he added, "yet."

He stood up. "How are you feeling?"

"I'll be up and about tomorrer," Harry Bones said. "What you got on your mind? You gonna take on as deputy—I mean private-like," he added quickly.

"I dunno," Clint said, feeling good toward the lawman. "I'll have to turn that over some. Meanwhile, tell me the whereabouts of Ephraim Crosby's house."

"You can't miss it. It's the biggest place in town—all brick, I mean the outside. Down thataways." He threw his thumb over his shoulder and canted his head at his visitor. "What's on your mind?"

"I'll let you know when I find out," Clint said. He walked to the doorway of the room and stopped. Turning, he hooked a thumb in his gunbelt and said, "Like to make a deal with you, marshal."

"Like what?" The tone was friendly as a sour apple.

"Like you help me and I'll help you."

The marshal of Sunshine Wells raised up then, digging his elbows into his bedding for support.

Squinting directly at the Gunsmith, he said, "Hell, ain't that what the two of us bin doin' for this past good while?"

Clint's grin was broad as he nodded and took his leave. It was sure true what Harry Bones had said, but he had wanted the marshal to actually say it.

Clint couldn't have put into words his reason for walking over to the Crosby house, but the impulse had been strong. Actually, he was trying to visualize the action of the murder, and it was therefore necessary to familiarize himself with the Crosby terrain.

The first thing he noted was the size of the brick house. In relation to the other buildings in Sunshine Wells this was truly a mansion. In the moonlight it struck an ominous note with him, somehow the house seemed shrouded. At first there were no lights showing —yet it was late—and this added to the atmosphere of gloom and mystery.

The large area surrounding the house had no fence to enclose it, and this seemed to Clint somewhat a sign of arrogance on the former owner's part. No person was expected to intrude. The path was set with flagstones and was wide enough to accommodate even a large rig with horses, and led to an imposing porch and front door.

There were two gardens, and he could see in the moonlight that they were properly cared for. He wondered if Crosby's wife took charge of them personally.

He didn't move in close to the house, skirting it as he studied the surrounding area. There were willows along one side of the large plot of land, and bushes on another, which he discovered led to a small creek at the rear of the house. There was a stable and two small outbuildings. A light shone dimly in the window of one, and he wondered if it was the servants' quarters. He assumed that a man of Ephraim Crosby's stature would have servants.

As he moved around the house he saw a lamplight in an upstairs window, presumably a bedroom. At last he completed his circle of the grounds and returned to where he had started. He had seen no one, but that wasn't surprising since the hour was late. He hadn't noticed anything unusual about the place, only noting that the distance from the building to the spot where Crosby's body was discovered was considerable. And the old man had somehow gotten himself there in the dead of night—without the help of his cane!

It was just as he was reflecting on this once again that he heard a sound coming from the house. The front door opened and someone came out. There was no light coming from the inside of the door entry so he was unable to get a clear view of the man. And at that moment he heard a horse and gig trotting up the street; it turned onto the path leading up to the house, stopped briefly for the large man to climb up, and then it was gone.

Clint waited, still keeping low in case there was anyone watching the place. He had been aware of such a possibility from the moment he first sighted the house, but now, realizing that there had indeed been a hurried furtiveness in the man leaving the house, he cautioned himself even more. A liaison in the middle of the night with Ephraim Crosby's widow? A man would surely exercise caution, and he might even have an accomplice or two covering his moves.

Clint wondered who the man was that would go to such pains. Why visit Lilly Crosby in the middle of the night? On the other hand, why not? There could be an easy answer to the question of motive. He had heard that Crosby's widow was a very attractive woman—and young, a lot younger than her husband had been.

• • •

It was his first day up and about, and as he walked down Main Street toward his office he was greeted right and left, at first to his gratification and eventually, as the number of how-de-do's and concerns for his health increased, to his irritation. But as he came to his office door, he remembered the warmth and restraint of Kerry Joyner's send-off from his house—the young, happy girl making him feel like a schoolboy, but in a good way. Harry Bones wished again that he could have had a daughter like Kerry.

On the other hand, Steve, his gray, impassive companion, had accompanied him to the office, and now sped past him as he opened the door and walked in.

He had brought a jar of milk with him, both for his coffee and the cat, and now, after lifting the window shades and letting in some light, he began to build a fire for coffee.

He ached, he felt somewhat older, and yet, in a strange way and at the same time, he felt younger. If pressed, he would have had to admit that he had enjoyed his stay in bed. The time to himself, the time with his nurse—simply the passage of time in which nothing had to be done—it was this that had healed him.

The morning brought a few visitors, mostly from the council, including Felix Porterhouse, though not Torb Mill. And then Sophie O'Govern suddenly surprised him, barging in with a huge smile, and a cloud of perfume that filled the entire room. Harry Bones noticed how Steve quickly departed through the door into the other part of the building. Sophie didn't stay long, she was all good wishes, and had brought him some food, which he didn't need.

"Do come and visit," she urged, as her sly eyes covered him.

"I surely will think about it, Sophie," he replied gallantly.

"Don't think, do!" And she departed, leaving a trail of raucous laughter.

The silence that followed was all the more precious to him. Yet there was still the sense of premonition with which he had started the day. Not in a bad way, but he felt that something was destined to happen. He supposed simply that it had to do with the men who had beaten him.

He poured himself another mug of coffee and sat back in the chair with only one arm. And he heard the light, hesitant step on the boardwalk outside in the street. In another moment there came a knock. He sat up in his chair, checked the six-gun at his hip. Who would be hesitant like that?

"It's open," he said in a loud voice, firm but not angry.

The thin, wiry man with the small face and wide eyes surprised him by taking his hat off as he entered and carefully shutting the door.

"My name is Abner Frolicher," he said. "I take it that you must be Marshal Bones."

"What kin I do fer you?"

"All right if I sit down, Marshal? I just wanted to ask you a few questions."

Someone had donated another chair to the office during his absence and now Harry Bones nodded to it. "Set," he said.

"My name is Abner Frolicher."

"You just told me that, mister. And anyways, I knew it already. Now tell me your business."

Abner sat down, nonplussed. "You knew my name?" His small eyebrows arched and his forehead wrinkled.

"Tell me your business." Harry Bones was beginning to feel impatient with his caller. But he cautioned himself. The man did write for the newspapers, and you never knew. "I happen to know you, just like I happen to know everybody," he said. "Since I happen to be the marshal of this here town."

A wan smile found its way into Abner's anxious expression and he softened. "Then you must know I am a newspaperman, a writer, I should say. Even—yes, an author." And he covered the little lie with an unctuous smile—to the great irritation of the marshal of Sunshine Wells, who remained glacially silent.

"I—uh—I am doing research on a book on one of the West's famous folk heroes," Abner said, swelling a little as his introduction developed. "And that's why I happen to be in Sunshine Wells."

"That how come you asked Tim Carstairs for a job on his paper?" Harry Bones countered sourly.

"No. No, that was something else. I am also looking for a job, but at the same time I'm doing research for a—well, possible book, or magazine article, or even a serial—on this man Adams, Clint Adams. Known as the Gunsmith. I'm sure you know who I'm talking about."

"So what do you want from me?"

As he said those words Harry Bones felt a sudden twinge inside him. It came from the place that had never left him—the place that tapped memory of "the old days." He looked carefully at Abner Frolicher. He would be too young to know anything, but he could have heard some things. That was the trouble with the damn news people, they were so goddam nosy. He sat forward a little, his insides readying for whatever might come. How many times he'd gone through this in the past years: the fear, the worry, and finally—as now, right now—the decision to scuttle it all. Because he knew how it could eat him.

Now, calmly, with his attention keened to the slightest shadings in the other man's voice, he waited.

"I just want to ask you if you can give me any background material regarding Adams, or any of the old gunmen, or present-day ones, that could be of use to me, to my article—or—book," he added, his voice trailing off as he saw the hard look coming into the marshal's face.

"Why don't you speak to Adams himself?"

"I plan to. But I was looking for background. For instance, as a lawman, can you tell me something of what it is like to have a famous gunfighter in your town?"

"About the same as having a famous newspaperman, I would reckon. I don't figger I can be much help to you, mister."

"Can I ask you one more question? Have you ever known, or encountered a famous gunfighter? I mean, somebody like Wild Bill Hickok, or Clay Allison, or Billy the Kid? Like that? Or maybe even . . ." Abner paused, searching his memory. And then he found it. "Maybe Cole Bonner?"

Harry Bones felt the closing in his guts then. But his

face was without expression as he said, "Sorry, I never knew a one of them gentlemen."

"Not a one? Well, all right then. Funny, one of my other interests has been to write something about Bonner."

"I never knew him."

"He's the only man ever escaped from an Oregon Boot, I've heard. At Folsom. Got clean away. He could still be alive."

"So could a lot of us," Harry Bones said sardonically. "Now I got work to do, mister."

Abner caught on fast, and almost jumped to his feet. "Sorry. Sorry to cut in on you, Marshal. And thank you for your time. Uh—can I use this material in my article? Our talk together?"

"No. You may not. Got that, Frolicher? No!"

"I got it. I've got it," Abner said and departed swiftly, his face flushed with embarrassment, puzzled why the marshal was suddenly so angry.

SEVEN

Felix Porterhouse, number-two man on the Sunshine Wells Council, and yearning to be number one, was worried. He had failed, and was not at all looking forward to facing Torb Mill, who had charged him with getting Clint Adams to come see him.

Felix had indeed confronted the man known as the Gunsmith as soon as he could locate him, and had said simply that Mr. Mill wanted to have a talk with him. Direct. Simple. Clear. Or so Felix Porterhouse had thought. Anyone with half a brain would have thought so, at any rate. And the fellow—Adams, could have simply asked what time, where, etcetera. But no.

"Then tell him he can ask," Adams had said. And without any expression on his face, he had continued walking down the street.

Felix, feeling as though he'd been put down even more adroitly than Torb was in the habit of doing, glared after the Gunsmith's retreating figure, And now, still furious, he faced Mill, standing like a schoolboy in front of the big desk, while Torb opened his mail.

"So you couldn't convince him, eh?" Torb was saying, without looking up at Felix.

"He just said that and walked off."

"Well, well . . ." After a rather long pause, "well . . ." Then, "Sit down, Felix. And stop fidgeting."

Porterhouse secured a chair and brought it closer to the desk and seated himself. And at that moment Torb looked up at him, finished with his mail.

"Felix, tell me what's been going on. First the general picture, and then details."

"Gandy's widow is still here. She's visited the cemetery each day. But I believe she'll be checking out in a day or two. So does Archie, the clerk at the Drover's Rest."

"And just what has Adams been up to? Snooping, I'll be bound."

Felix nodded, grateful for the change in Torb's tone. "He has been all over the place, down to the cribs, into all the saloons, everywhere. God knows what kind of story he's getting together. He's surely working for the widow."

"Well, as we know, he's seen the widow Gandy more than once. And I must say, she is—uh—a fine piece of womanhood." Torb's voice had deepened as he said this, and Felix took note of it. Nor did the number-two man miss the sparkle in the other's eyes. "He's trying to find something that would prove Gandy was innocent. Well—he won't!"

Felix felt a great sense of relief.

"What about the wagon and the whiskey?"

"Operation done as you wished, sir!" Felix, suddenly in a playful mood, saluted, snapping his heels together, and this brought a grin to Torb's beefy face.

With just the correct measure of hesitancy, Felix now said, "I, of course, don't inquire into anything I am not supposed to know, Torb, but as we are both members of the council, I do wonder what this Indian business is all about."

"You wonder?"

"About the fake attack on the stagecoach, for example. The boys sure made a mess of it. And this thing with the whiskey. Runs-His-Horses doesn't want any whiskey in his camp. Nor guns. So?" He spread his hands, eyebrows raised, and shrugged, letting the question hang. "There could be big trouble with the Shoshone."

Felix was counting on Torb's vanity. He knew Mill loved to explain things to those whom he considered less smart than himself. He loved to display his swift ability to size a situation, a person, and to manipulate as required.

"Simple," he said now, pointing his sharp nose directly at Felix. "I had thought to scare off Mrs. Gandy. There was the chance she might ask embarrassing questions about her husband, and so on. But that damned Gunsmith fellow just happened to be there on the spot. But—never mind. It's all working out as I've planned."

Felix remained silent in the face of what he considered at best a half truth. Granted, the false attack on the stage with the made-up drunken Indians could have scared away the widow, but there seemed to him to be another, deeper reason behind it all. After all, what about the whiskey wagon and the crate of rifles?

But Torb was saying something more now. "On the other hand, we were lucky. It just so happened that one of the passengers was a newspaperman. And as we all know, the men who scribble the news know how to spread it, and they are also good at digging it out. I confess I spotted that man Frobisher or Frinlicker, whatever—right off. He tried for a job here in town and Carstairs reported it to me. What luck, eh?"

"You mean, let him have the information you want him to have, is that it?"

"Well, what do you think we've been doing?" Torb's pleasant expression had suddenly turned to ice. "You ask too many questions, Porterhouse."

"I . . ." Felix had lost his breath in the face of the other's vigorous switch from friendliness to attack.

"I am not speaking to you now in your capacity as a member of the town council," Mill went on, "but as my assistant—I should say, one of my assistants—in a very private enterprise. An enterprise, and let me repeat it again and again, about which nobody—repeat nobody, nobody, *nobody*—must even suspect the slightest thing!"

"I understand, Torb. I understand."

"Then we shall drop the subject."

A long pause followed while Felix stared at a large water stain on the wall, and Torb Mill inspected his fingernails.

Outside in the street a dog was barking.

Presently Torb finished with his fingernails, touched

the end of his nose with his forefinger, and said, "Let us get to council business now."

The dog was still barking out in the street.

That Abner Frolicher failed to get a job on the Sunshine Wells *Clarion* came as no surprise to the wizened young man. And indeed, in a strange way he felt relieved. The point was, things were normal, as expected; he had failed again. And in this he knew a kind of ease, security. He wasn't afraid, and he wasn't anxious. He was in fact, in his usual place—on the outside looking in. And then, too, he had bigger game in mind. He had the story of the Gunsmith swiftly collecting at his fingertips as he watched the subject of his "masterpiece," and mentally turned phrase after phrase recording brisk and daring action: as for instance the passage at arms at the Screaming Eagle. Incredible!

Encouraged by the drama that he saw unfolding before his eyes, he went so far as to rent a horse at the livery and engage in a short ride in order to familiarize himself with the animal, which was obviously an essential part of the western story. He was all but totally discouraged after the second day on his short forays out of town on a dappled gray mare that was gaunted enough to show every rib through her aged hide, yet with still enough life in her to dislodge her rider twice the first day and twice again on the next. But Abner's chief character trait came to the fore, and he persevered— in the face of ridicule from some small boys who bore witness to his failure as a horseman—not to mention the physical pain he suffered all over his small body.

Abner persevered and the mare and he struck up a sort of relationship. On the third day she tired a bit of crowhopping, but Abner remained in the saddle. That same afternoon he rode farther away from the town, following a trail that he had seen Clint Adams take. He had decided that the time had come for him to reintroduce himself to the Gunsmith, reminding him of his presence on the stagecoach that Clint had saved from Indian ambush.

He didn't know it then, but he was to discover that the events that followed would make up the main drive of his proposed book about the Gunsmith.

Clint had been aware all along that Abner Frolicher was watching him. He suspected that the man was seeking information for his own use. Jackie Gandy had told him Frolicher was a newspaperman, plus Clint had spotted him in the bar when he'd backed down the Double Bar B men, and had also remembered seeing him in the stagecoach, and swiftly and accurately concluded that the wingy little man with the mild, nut-brown eyes and worried frown could not possibly have anything at all to do with the business he was investigating. Abner Frolicher could be only one thing—and one only. He had to be just exactly what he was.

But the Gunsmith didn't dwell on it. He had important matters to occupy him, and there was something he felt drawn to at the particular moment; in fact, there were two things. One was the need to pay a visit to the Shoshone camp, and the other, which was much more difficult to articulate as a clear thought, was simply that he wanted to ride out to the area where the drunken

Indians had chased the stage. He didn't know why, but he just felt the strong necessity to take a look, a second look.

It was a day that seemed longer than usual. There were days like that, Clint knew, days of endless blue sky and the clean, fresh smell of his horse moving under him. And the smell of the sage, the rustle of cottonwood leaves, the heated keening sound of the grass as he rode over it under the hot sun. And the sense of his own self inhabiting his body, living that keen alertness that he had known all his life. Now, watching an eagle sweep the great arc of sky just ahead of him, he knew that bird had to feel it, too; that great freedom he felt singing and soaring in him.

And than as he rode across the open prairie he found himself thinking about the Crosby killing and how that single act had affected so many people; and especially how it had touched the life of Jackie Gandy. But there was more to that simple killing than met anybody's eye. For it had exposed a number of things. Above all, it had exposed Crosby; and he had the feeling that more was going to be revealed. Somehow, in some way, he felt certain it had something to do with the Shoshone.

Only what? If there was a plot of some kind behind the killing, a plot that involved the Indians, what could it possibly be? Somebody wanting their land? Surely that was one of the main difficulties between the Indians and the white men—the discovery of gold on land that had been assigned to the Indians, or the wish to run railroad track through treaty land, or simply the desire to move the redmen away—far away, no matter where, but just to get rid of them, the only good Indian being "a dead one."

Only a few moments after these thoughts, he reached the open place where the drunken braves had attacked the stagecoach, and his whole theory was thrown out. The strange thing was that while he was astonished at what he discovered, he was even more surprised when he realized that somehow he had known all along that it was so.

Some time had certainly passed, but it hadn't rained in the interim, and some of the hoof prints were still clear. Enough to tell him that the horses chasing the stage had been shod. It was then he realized that something had been nudging him all along, ever since that day; likely something in the way those "Indians" had been riding. And he had sensed it, but it hadn't worked out in his thinking. Now there was no question in his mind that those "Indians" had not been red at all—they were white men.

Looking up then from where he'd been squatting in order to examine the prints, he saw a man riding toward him. It was the man from the stagecoach. It was Abner Frolicher.

Harry Bones found himself mending quickly. A lifetime of hard knocks proved to be standing him well in his later years. And he knew he was going to need every ounce of his new strength now in the days that were coming.

He was expecting him, and there he was. Torb Mill was just as forceful as ever when he walked into the marshal's office.

"Glad to hear—and now to see—that you're on the mend, Harry." He held out his hand, hearty, open, and sincere to anyone who might have taken a glance in the direction of this particular tableau.

But Harry Bones hadn't been a lawman and a few other things all his years without learning something. He read Torb Mill like he was carved in stone.

Harry's face was impassive as he returned the handshake, using his left hand.

"How's that right one?" Torb asked, loaded with concern and sincerity.

"It's comin'." The fact was, his right hand and arm were just fine, but Harry Bones knew that from now on he was going to need all the advantage he could get. So let Mill—and any others—think he was still stove up. That was the way he was going to handle it.

"I dropped by with something besides wanting to wish you well, Harry."

"I figgered that out already, Torb." And Harry Bones savored the sour smile that took over Mill's oily directness. "What is it you want?"

Torb cleared his throat, sniffed, regained his composure. "I want to know if you've seen Adams recently. I mean in the last twenty-four hours, say."

"Nope."

"I think you should be keeping an eye on that man. You, of course, know his reputation. Fast gun, and all that. The point is, we have to have law and order here. I know you agree with me. But then you've been out of things a while, and haven't been able to function as well as we—both of us—would have liked."

"What's Adams got to do with that? It wasn't Adams

beat on me. It was Jesse and Heavy John Bearing's boys.''

''True. True.''

Torb Mill had drawn up the chair that was for some reason standing quite deserted in the middle of the almost bare room, and now he sat down and crossed one leg over the other, his eyes bearing down on the marshal, who regarded his visitor calmly.

''Then what about Bert Smiles?'' Mill asked suddenly, almost throwing the question at the lawman.

Harry took out a quirly and lighted it. He took his time, while his sour eyes remained on Torb, even while he struck the wooden lucifer with his thumbnail, one-handed.

''You know what about Bert. I keep him as deputy number one, on account of I can't get anybody else—not at the pay that's offered,'' he added. ''And number two, Bert's easy to pump on the local news.'' He took a drag on the quirly and then said, ''How come you keep Bert on *your* payroll, Mill?''

He watched it hit the other man. And Mill realized the futility of denial.

He said, ''Same reason as you, I guess, Harry.''

''We know where we stand then.''

''Where?''

''Pretty directly now I will be riding out to the Double Bar B.''

''And . . .?''

''With a warrant for Jesse and the boys.''

Torb Mill looked down at the back of his fingers and then turned his eyes directly to Harry Bones. ''And what if they refuse the invitation, Harry?''

"Then somebody's gonna take up permanent residence right quick."

Torb took a deep breath and let it out. " 'Course I don't rightly care what happens to Bearing's boys, Harry. I am just asking the question. Like that." And he smiled.

"Torb, you're full of shit."

Harry Bones said it slow and easy, without any anger, and Torb Mill remembered again how he'd ordered him to apologize to Joyner's daughter. The man had changed. No question about it. Was it his wife's death that finally got to him, Or what?

"I know all about your connection with Heavy John Bearing and the Double Bar B, Torb. I don't care one way or the other. But don't try handing me that kind of cowshit. You don't care! That'll be the day when something goes on in this town and Torb Mill don't care. But get this: You do your own business, whatever it is, I don't care. See? Only those sons of bitches not only messed with me, they messed with the law. And they are going to get their fucking asses griddled! But I will try going by the law—to start with!"

There was a big grin on Mill's face as he heard the marshal out. And when silence had fallen again Mill said, "Harry, calm yourself." The smile broadened as he stood up. "Don't get so excited. The boys didn't mean any harm, I'm sure. I'll have Bearing talk to them. Take it slow, Harry." And now the smile reached its limit, and suddenly Torb's face was hard and sharp as a straight razor. "Or should I say 'Cole.' "

In the terrible silence that followed neither man heard or even saw the gray cat crossing from where he'd been taking the sunlight at the window to where the marshal of Sunshine Wells was sitting in the chair with one arm.

The silence lasted for as long as it took Steve the cat to lick one paw.

"That ain't gonna work anymore, Torb," Harry said.

"I wouldn't be so sure," Mill said easily. "Of course, unless you prefer Folsom to Sunshine Wells."

Harry Bones didn't even blink. His voice was easy as a fistful of four aces as he said, "There is a way to find out, Mill."

"Keep his head up!" Clint shouted as the chunky little roan started to crowhop.

Abner Frolicher, already having regretted that he'd decided against the crowbait mare and had asked the hostler at Hoke's for the blue roan, was grabbing at his saddle horn, trying to keep his legs tight on the barrel of the tough gelding, and feeling as though he was going to toss his entire stomach in the next moment. He was also sure he'd smashed one of his testicles.

The horse had started to spin and already Abner had lost one stirrup, and suddenly the animal sunfished and his rider landed flat on his back in a clump of sage.

The horse finished out his bucking, and Clint swiftly dismounted Duke and walked over to where the little newspaperman lay coughing and gasping, the breath actually knocked out of him. Seeing that he wasn't hurt too badly, Clint caught the roan and led him back to his rider.

Clint was watching Duke, however. The big black horse was veering away from something not far from

his view, with his ears out to the sides, filled with
caution.

"What is it, Duke, boy? A rattler?"

Indeed it was, and in the next moment Clint drew
and fired, the bullet ending the life of the rattlesnake in
an explosion of blood, bone, flesh, and presumably,
spirit.

Abner Frolicher was still trying to catch his breath
and lay on his back, croaking, unable to articulate a
single word to express his pain, anger, frustration, or
possibly even prayer. His recent adversary, meanwhile,
was cropping the short buffalo grass only a few feet
away as though nothing untoward had happened.

Clint holstered his gun. "Well, that'll bring 'em
running if nothing else will," he said.

Abner coughed out something incomprehensible.

Clint took his sound to mean the word "Who?" and
he answered him accordingly. "The Shoshone. I wanted
to meet up with them, only on my terms, not like this."

He stood looking down at the small man who was
now struggling to sit up. "You all right?"

The former rider gargled something unintelligible.
He had managed to get to his feet. Clint didn't offer
any assistance, knowing that it would be inappropriate
either to spoil such a dude, or run the risk of humiliat-
ing him. A long while later, Abner was to appreciate
the Gunsmith's attitude. For the moment, however, he
almost came another cropper by stepping into a pile of
fresh horse manure as he started to walk toward the
roan, and skidded to his knees.

"Jesus H. Christ!" the little man suddenly roared.
"What next!"

Clint had difficulty controlling his laughter. "What do you expect, for crying out loud, following me about all over the place!" He spoke with mock seriousness.

"I wasn't following you *everywhere*," cried Abner. "I was just watching you to get to know you."

"For whom? Who hired you? Or was this your own bright notion?"

"Nobody hired me. I followed you because I want to write about you. That's why."

"Christ! What kind of an asshole thing is that!"

"You are famous," Abner said, drawing himself up now as his normal breathing returned, and with it his voice and the realization that he had not broken anything. "The people back East want to read about the deeds of the heroes of the Great American West!"

"Bullshit!"

"Not bullshit! It is a fact, and indeed you could even make some money in places like Chicago and Philadelphia and such—lecturing to large audiences. Lots of westerners have done that. And they've cleaned up."

"I don't happen to be 'lots of westerners,' " Clint said harshly. "Now we'd better get out of here. The Shoshone might not be too friendly—I mean, if it's some renegade band we run into—so I guess I'm stuck with you." And he added, as he stepped into his stirrup, "For the moment, leastways." When he was in the saddle he watched the other man struggling to mount.

The blue roan kept circling away so that Abner couldn't swing up and over; the saddle wasn't beneath him, and twice he all but fell.

"Hold your off rein and he can't turn then," Clint instructed. "Hold it tight, plus a handful of mane. Get a good grip. And swing up and over close to him, not wide.''

Abner tried again and this time he made it. He beamed at the Gunsmith. ''By George, it works.''

''You could write a book about that,'' the Gunsmith said.

''About climbing aboard a feisty horse.''

''About getting something right.''

Clint kicked the big black gelding into a brisk canter as the man on the blue roan followed.

EIGHT

It was about the middle of the afternoon when they splashed across the little creek and saw the thin columns of smoke rising above the cottonwood trees.

The Indian camp was well concealed, but Clint could smell the cooking, felt the different vibration in the atmosphere as they approached, and was only waiting for someone to appear to challenge them.

"What is this place?" Abner Frolicher asked, pulling up beside Duke who, at Clint's signal, had come to a stop and was now rubbing his long nose against his extended foreleg, while his bit jingled in the quiet air.

"It's their camp."

"The Indians?"

Clint caught the alarm in his companion's voice. "The Shoshone," he said calmly. "Just don't say or do anything. Especially don't make any fast moves."

He had hardly spoken when a man on horseback came out of the trees just ahead of them.

Clint held up his hand in the sign of peace. He

couldn't see but the one Shoshone, but he knew there were more surrounding them in the trees.

"I am Adams," he said. "I've come to talk with Runs-His-Horses." He signed as he spoke the few words he knew in Shoshone.

The warrior, who sat a hammerhead sorrel horse, answered him in English. "You are friend to Runs-His-Horses?"

"Long ago, many moons . . ." He made a counting motion with his hand. "Long . . ." And pointed with his finger circling in front of him. "At Border Creek I talked with Runs-His-Horses. I was scout for army then. Now I am not a scout. I come as a friend."

"You stay." The warrior moved his hand in front of him so that Clint and Abner would know there were other men in the trees.

"I know they are there," Clint said. "I hear them."

"You have good ears for a white man," the Indian said, starting to turn his horse.

"And your young men make noise—for Indians," Clint said with a smile.

The face looked at him impassively. Clint had said what he had, not to put any insult into the conversation, but to let the Shoshone know that he was no greener.

"You wait."

He was back shortly and signaled that they were to follow him.

The camp was deep in the trees, completely hidden, save for the wisps of smoke rising above, which could only be seen by the practiced eye. It lay between two creeks, and on the far side there was a meadow from which came the sound of grazing bulls as Clint and Abner followed their guide through the camp.

Here the smell of cooking was stronger, and they saw women and children, all standing still, watching as they rode by. They had stopped their work or play and stood with expressionless faces.

The camp was pitched in the form of a horseshoe with the open end facing the east where the sun would rise. They stopped in front of the lodge that was most central and their guide told them to dismount and enter.

Chief Runs-His-Horses was seated in front of a small fire. The guide indicated where they should sit. No words were spoken. The guide retired and they were left alone with Runs-His-Horses.

It was silent in the lodge. Even Abner was still, Clint noted. The silence filled the entire lodge, so strong it was almost audible.

Now Runs-His-Horses reached forward and lifted his pipe from its special place by the fire. Carefully he prepared the tobacco, and then, taking an ember from the fire—actually a wooden chip, there being no more buffalo in that land—he drew on the pipe, lighting it.

He passed it to Clint, who smoked, and then passed it to Abner who almost choked, but manfully controlled himself with the tears streaming down his cheeks.

"What is it you want?" Runs-His-Horses said after he had returned the pipe to its special place.

Clint had been wondering if the chief remembered him, and had decided not to ask, but to let it come as it would—or would not.

"I am Adams," he said. "This is my friend Abner. I have come to ask you about the whiskey wagon that I saw a while ago not far from here. I have heard, Runs-His-Horses, that you do not allow whiskey in your lodge or camp; but there were white men who brought it. It was down by the southern creek." And he pointed the direction.

The chief was silent for such a long time that Clint wondered if he was going to reply. But at last he spoke.

"The wagon was brought by white men. But I did not want it. Many times the white men have tried to sell me whiskey. And I have refused. It is not for my people."

"I have heard that, Runs-His-Horses. Many white men know that you are against the whiskey."

"The Burning Water is for the white man, not for the Shoshone."

"But, still, there was whiskey brought."

The chief took a moment longer to reply to this, but at last he said, "The white traders wanted to give us this whiskey. I still refused. They wanted to give us guns. I refused. Many times I have refused the whiskey. Now they try to give us guns."

"So, it is true about the guns."

"Whiskey and guns. I refused. My head men were all in agreement. No one here wanted guns or whiskey. We are at peace with the White Father."

"And so what happened then?" Clint asked. "The wagon was there. I saw it. I smelled the whiskey. I even saw some of the white men, though they did not see me. They were returning from your camp."

"I know. They left the wagon near our camp, even though we refused it. I then sent my warriors to hide it. For they were bad men. Gray men. What you call out . . . law. And they wanted us to have trouble with the pony soldiers. I do not know.'' He paused. ''That is all I know.''

The chief's silence enveloped everything in the lodge. Clint again felt it as something quite tangible; as though at the conclusion of what he had to say, Runs-His-Horses had returned deeply into himself.

They continued to sit there for a while. After what seemed a considerable time the flap of the tent was pulled back and the warrior who had brought them entered.

''Come,'' he said.

As Clint rose to leave, he felt the chief's eyes on him. Suddenly Runs-His-Horses spoke.

''I remember you, Adams. At Border Creek. Go now and tell the other whites how the whiskey and guns came here—as gifts! They are buried down by the crossing after you come to the one called Pony Butte; just to the north of that place there are three cotton-woods and a bullberry bush. A big rock covers the boxes. I do not want them. Take them!''

''I will send men for them,'' Clint said and he ducked through the tent opening and out into the evening, which was just beginning to fall through the trees.

Neither he nor Abner spoke as they rode in the twilight toward Sunshine Wells. It was clear to Clint that his companion's silence bore testimony to their meeting with a special man. He had met others such as Runs-His-Horses, other Indians. Defeated, vanquished— but only in the world of guns and killing. In the world of the sun, the moon, the stars, and the animals, the birds, the air, and the water some men like Runs-His-Horses would still live. Of that he was sure.

And now as he rode toward Sunshine Wells he could still feel something of what he had felt in the chief's lodge. He had felt that before, with some of the old Indians and even some white men; and in special places in the beautiful country. There was nothing like it. Anywhere.

Saturday night in Sunshine Wells was a lively time; that meant the cribs, the saloons, the gaming tables were in brisk action. Down in the Cabbage Patch, Sophie O'Govern's girls were busy. Mostly it was the Double Bar B men from Heavy John Bearing's outfit up on the North Fork. Jesse Ollinger and Dink Wilson were making more noise than the rest of the bunch put together. Sophie didn't care. She was raking in the money.

All the girls were working hard, as Sophie pointed out. And she reiterated her favorite phrase, that none of her prices had gone up. The only thing that did go up in her establishment were penises, and Sophie boasted that there was nary a limp one that left her house dissatisfied.

"Every man gets his dippin's," was how the lady put it. "The O'Govern House has the best in the West! And don't nobody forget it!"

It must have been midnight, or even later when Heavy John Bearing put in an appearance. He stepped through the doorway, with his Stetson on the back of his head and his hands hooked into his gunbelt. Sophie had always said privately that the man had the biggest feet she'd ever seen in her life.

This night she felt something different about Heavy John. First of all he didn't normally come when his boys were there, unless it was to haul them back to the ranch. And then, too, there was something funny in his attitude. But she let it pass. Fact was, she didn't know Heavy John all that well. Whenever he did come on girl business he always wanted the same one—a Mexican girl with enormous breasts. Nina.

Tonight he didn't ask for Nina. And he didn't seem to have come to take his men back to the Double Bar B. But the place was rocking, and Sophie finally paid him no mind, just let him drink in the corner of the room and talk to some of the men.

It got later. Heavy John had been there over an hour and while he'd had plenty to drink, he hadn't wanted Nina or anyone else for that matter. And then at one point, maybe one o'clock, the clientele began to thin out. And soon there was only Heavy John and his men.

When Sophie came back into the front room, the singing and dancing had stopped. Elbows Kinton, the fiddler, had departed, and the Double Bar B men were standing about or sitting; in fact not even talking much. There were four of them including Heavy John.

"You boys look like you need a little action to liven you up," Sophie said, and later she told how she'd had that funny feeling in her right then.

"The girls all upstairs, Sophie?" Heavy John asked.

"That they are. Asleep likely," Sophie said. "All fucked out."

And when she saw she hadn't raised a laugh she felt something tighten in her.

Heavy John Bearing was staring at her. He had a big

face, huge shoulders, and hands that could bust a calf for branding like it was a toy.

"What's up, boys?" Sophie managed to steady her hand as she lifted her glass of whiskey. "About time for some shut-yer-eyes, ain't it?"

Heavy John didn't answer her. He nodded to one of the men, who started toward the door. "And you, too," Heavy John said to another. "One in front, one in back; and you watch the horses," he told the third man.

"What's going on, hey?"

"We're going to have a little talk, Sophie," Heavy John said and he stood up, looking even bigger, Sophie thought. "You an' me an' Jesse here. We're gonna talk."

"Sure. Sure, John. What about? What you want to talk about? You want a drink? It's on the house. Jesse?"

"We want to know about this Adams, this feller calls hisself Gunsmith."

Sophie put her glass down on top of the piano. "Hell, he's just a man come here once. Didn't ask for a girl. Just wanted to talk."

"What did you talk about?"

"Nothing special. He just asked about the town. The people. He's a stranger. Just was lonesome, I reckoned."

"Who did he ask about?"

"Nobody special."

Suddenly Jesse's fist swung into the middle of her back. He had been out of sight behind her, while Heavy John had been speaking, and she was totally unprepared for the blow. She went crashing into the sofa.

"Tell me what he wanted to know. There's more of

that.'' Heavy John Bearing's voice was soft as Sophie struggled to her feet. ''Don't make noise. We don't want the girls down here.''

Sophie's anger was what saved her. It drowned the pain. And suddenly, without the slightest warning, she stepped forward and slammed the palm of her hand against Jesse's grinning face. Turning, and with her back to him she bent, bringing her arm and hand down and back in a chopping gesture—like a scythe—and smashed him in the crotch.

So swift had her action been that neither of the men could accept it. Heavy John broke into a laugh, while Jesse cried out in pain. Nothing could have been more of a surprise to the two Double Bar B men than the old woman's speed and resourcefulness, not to mention her courage.

''By Jesus, Sophie, I'll bet you got balls in your pants, and here we never knew it all along!'' roared Heavy John.

''You fuckers get yerself and your tin balls out of my house. I mean right now!'' She was gasping from her exertions and indignation. ''And don't never come the fuck back!''

Whereupon Heavy John Bearing backhanded her across the face and she staggered.

''Shut up,'' he said. ''That was funny what you did to Jesse. We'll let that pass. But hear me tell you this! That feller Adams comes here again I want to know it. I mean right now. I want to know what he does, what he asks.''

Sophie stood small before him. She had shot her

bolt. And now she was once again her age. Her moment of glory had come—and gone.

"He asked about the night that feller broke jail; when
you came for your men that night."

"What did you tell him?"

"I told him you came and got your men and that was
all I know."

"What else did you tell him?"

"He asked if I heard anything. I said yes—just like the
whole town must of heard the yelling and shooting and
all that went on. Nothing else. Goddammit, not another
fucking thing!" And she put her face in her hands and
sobbed.

"I want to know if he ever comes here again and if
he does, what he asks. You mind that now!"

Sophie dropped her hands and stood facing Heavy
John. "Go fuck yerself," she said.

"You don't tell anybody what happened tonight.
Else . . ." He pointed his thumb toward the ceiling.
"A few of them won't look so good anymore."

He had her then. It was not necessary to say anything
more.

When they were gone she walked to the back of the
short hallway and lifted her eyes to the full-length
mirror. She looked at the tears that stood like stones
before her pitiless gaze. Her hair hung all over her, the
painted face was a smear. She was shaking.

Sophie O'Govern stood there where she was. She
straightened herself, still shaking. She ran her palms
over her hips, touched at a shoulder strap beneath her
cerise-colored gown. She pressed her lips together, trying
to bring color through the smeared paint. Her fingers

touched one large lobe where the earring was missing.
She dabbed at the trickle of blood coming from her
nose. She saw that she would need powder to cover the
discoloration that was already blue; and yes, a drink
because it was painful.

She stood before herself for another moment, until
the tears dried.

And she said, "Go fuck yerselfs, you prick-lickers!
Go fuck yerselfs!"

Jackie Gandy wasn't at the Drover's Rest when
Clint inquired at the desk. There was a new man filling in as room clerk, while the regular was having
lunch.

"But she's still checked in here," Clint said.

The room clerk nodded. His look was somber. Something about him provoked the Gunsmith to ask a question.

"Where is she?" And the tone of his voice demanded an answer.

"She got cut from glass. She's at Doc Joyner's; or
would be by now, I reckon."

"Cut? How? What happened? Tell me fast!" He
leaned forward, his eyes pressing the little man, who in
fact took a step backward.

"Someone, some kids maybe, threw a rock at her
window this morning early, and she got cut."

"How bad?"

"She's all right, mister. I don't know anything about
it."

"You mean you don't want to know anything about
it," snapped Clint, gripping the man with his eyes. "I

will be back, and I will expect you to answer whatever questions I might have.''

By now the room clerk was frightened. ''Mister, I'm just filling in for Hank; he's the regular. I don't know anything. Only that Mrs. Gandy, she went off to the Doc again, about a hour ago.''

Clint was already at the door as the clerk finished speaking.

He found Harry Bones in Fabio Joyner's office along with Jacqueline. He immediately spotted the patch just above her eye.

''I just got back, heard the news,'' Clint said.

She was obviously relieved to see him; her smile of welcome told him.

''It was like before,'' Harry Bones explained. ''Only this time it wasn't just words. It was also a big hunk of rock. In fact, three rocks. Close. Real close.''

''It just missed the eye,'' Joyner said. ''Real lucky.''

''Any idea who it was?'' Clint turned to the marshal. ''I thought you had Smiles watching the place. Your deputy.''

''I did. I threatened the—the man,'' he said, changing his vocabulary to suit the presence of Jackie Gandy, ''since I still couldn't get a deputy worth a hill of beans. Thought he'd learned something. And I will say this for him. He didn't just step aside. They knocked him out cold. He's got a head fit for a hoss.''

''Where is he?''

''At my office. I keep him there now. Got a cot. I want my eye on him!''

Clint quickly sensed the difference in Harry Bones. Something had come to the man. It was clear, abso-

lutely clear that he was talking to a different Harry
Bones. It was as though something that had been lost in
the man had come back. Clint found himself grinning at
the marshal, who just looked at him, canting his head a
little, and not saying anything more.

"You'll still be shaky for a while," Doc Joyner was
saying to Jacqueline. "But there isn't much blood loss.
Might slow you down, but not serious. As I told you
earlier, it won't need stitching." He looked at Clint. "I
saw her immediately after it happened; this now is
really a checkup to be sure." He turned back to Jackie
Gandy. "You were fortunate, Mrs. Gandy."

"Well, I must say that's not quite how I felt when
those rocks came flying into my room with all that
glass." Her tone was dry, without any self-pity, Clint
noted.

Dr. Joyner smiled wryly. "If I might just say what
I'm . . . sayin' . . . you could have had serious dam-
age. Your whole face could've been cut up. You could
have gotten a sliver of glass in your eye, in your neck,
meaning into your throat, or even elsewhere on your
body, in some vital place. I repeat, you got off lucky
and there shouldn't be any permanent scar."

She smiled suddenly. "I'm sorry. I was too quick.
It's one of my failings. And I apologize. I know you
were reassuring me. But at this point in my life, I'm not
too concerned with looks. What I am concerned with is
my husband. His name. I intend to clear his name. And
this has spurred me to redouble my efforts. I will not be
stopped. I know—and I am sure that you know, too,
yes, you also, Marshal Bones—that Todd Gandy was
innocent. And it will be proven!"

Harry Bones opened his hands, moving his head slightly in a questioning gesture. "But the evidence—"

"You know that's fake," Clint said, cutting in. "Look, if the real killer found Gandy drunk—" He looked quickly at Jackie. "I know he didn't drink, at least not heavily. You told me that and I believe you. I'm just saying *suppose*. Like it's claimed. Suppose Todd Gandy was drunk. Out! Out cold! Why couldn't the real killer have packed him over to where he'd knifed Crosby himself and drop him there. Easy as pie!"

"Could be." The marshal sniffed, pursed his lips in thought, and squinted at the ceiling.

"And the jailbreak," Clint pursued. "It smells."

Again, the marshal of Sunshine Wells was offering his hands, palms up. "What can I say? You've got Bert's statement. Sworn statement. Yes, I know he's not the most honest man I've ever met, but he was there; he was guarding Gandy." He turned toward Jackie quickly. "I'm sorry, ma'am, that we go into all this in front of you."

"Don't mind it. I'm used to it; and I am bound, sworn, to clearing Todd's name. You men talk it out. After all, it's perfectly clear to me."

"How was Bert Smiles when you saw him, Doc?" Clint asked, suddenly catching at something that had been going through his thoughts. "I mean, after Gandy was shot."

"Seemed all right. Angry. But then I didn't see Bert till the day after, when he was giving evidence."

"But everybody told me he'd been pistol-whipped. And now I recollect I never even saw a bruise on his head when I first met up with him. He must have required medical treatment, though, at the time.''

"He didn't get any from me. Matter of fact, he did have a slight black-and-blue mark on the side of his face when I spoke to him the day after Gandy was shot.'' He looked over at Jacqueline and dropped his eyes. "Boys, maybe we ought to talk about this later.''

"Wait a minute!'' It was Jacqueline Gandy. "Clint here is asking about the fact that everyone said this man, the deputy, was whipped with a pistol, and suggesting that if that had been the case he would have needed medical care. But he didn't get any medical care, and nobody, none of you gentlemen, seems to have seen any sign of such an attack. I'm assuming what you mean when you say 'pistol whip' that it means beating someone with a heavy firearm.''

Harry Bones was the first to speak in the sudden silence that greeted her outburst. "I got to say, for me I took it like a saying, maybe exaggerated, the way a man will do when he's had a rough time. Now I think back on it, the shock on all of us—well, no one was really thinking any too clear.'' He sniffed, rubbed the side of his nose with his thumb. "I think I'll have me another talk with that gentleman.''

"I think that's a good idea,'' Clint said ominously. "So let's leave it now.''

When they left Doc Joyner's office Clint offered to walk Jackie to the Drover's Rest, and she accepted.

"It's a big strain on you,'' he was saying as they walked toward the hotel. "And I want you to know your courage does not go unnoticed—not by Joyner or the marshal, and for sure not by myself.''

"Thank you," she said softly.

When they reached the hotel she didn't seem in any hurry to go inside.

"I'd like to have dinner, supper, if you feel up to it," Clint said. "Only I can't be sure when I can make it a real invitation. Right now I've got a lot to look into."

"You've done so much for me already."

"Keeps me young," he said with a grin. "And it isn't just for you. It's good sometimes to help keep the record straight."

"You mean, you're also trying to help Marshal Bones?"

He nodded. "I guess so."

"Is he an old friend of yours?" And then she added quickly. "Sorry. I take it back; I'm just being nosy."

"No, I wouldn't say he was an old friend," Clint said, "I did know somebody once who I think knew him a little. But that was a good while back. And I'm not sure."

Then, touching the brim of his Stetson he said, "I'll be back with a definite invitation."

When he found out what had happened to Sophie O'Govern, the Gunsmith almost forgot the role he had chosen to play. For several moments he had the thought to saddle Duke, ride out to the Double Bar, and exact full vengeance on Heavy John Bearing and his boys. But he managed to calm down after talking to Sophie, whose spirits were as high as her courage.

"I will even it with the sons-of-bitches," she promised.

"How?" Clint asked. "You can't go up against those men."

"You don't know everything, young feller, and that's a fact," Sophie said shrewdly. She had recovered herself and even her face had nearly returned to normal. "You men! See, you all got your head in the air or in some gal's pants. But you don't see what really goes on in this world."

"Tell me, Sophie."

They were having a drink in the O'Govern parlor.

"You know they got this place watched," Sophie began.

"Spotted the three of them on my way in."

"They'll be in here wanting to know what you said, what you wanted to know; all like that."

"So we'll have a story ready for them."

"That's what I know."

"So how would you get even with them? I am just asking the question. And how is it we men don't know so much as you women?"

"Grin like you want," she snapped at him. "But you men are one thing with a hard on, and somethin' quite different after you've had it. Men don't get led by their nose, but by their cock. Any damn fool knows that."

"So? Women, too."

"That's for sure," Sophie agreed, apparently unaware how she was denying the validity of her claim about men. "But that sonofabitch, or any one of them sons-of-bitches mess with me again I'll wait till he's into one of the girls and I'll bust his balls. I mean for good."

Clint chuckled. "How would you do that, Sophie?"

"Easy," she said with a sly grin. "Feller's humpin'
away he ain't gonna notice somebody slipping into the
room, until"—she made a snatching motion with her
hand—"I grabs his balls and yanks 'em off the
sonofabitch. I mean it!" she insisted, while the Gunsmith roared with laughter at her acting out the scene.

"Or I'll sic some of them drunk red devils onto
'em," she went on. It was obvious now to Clint that
she was well into her booze.

"So what about those Indians?" he asked, just to see
if she'd heard anything. "You know about their getting
whiskey, and maybe guns?"

"Yup. I've been hearing that talk this while. And I
sure wouldn't be surprised."

"Where did you hear it?" Clint asked, his interest
suddenly spurred.

"Heard it from the Double Bar B men and some
others." She leaned forward. "My customers tell me
and the girls everything." And she beamed smugly at
him and giggled.

"Who else told you that?"

"Told me what?" She hiccuped suddenly and took a
swift drink.

"Told about the Indians drinking and so on."

"And so on? And so on, you calls it! Why them red
devils is like as not to burn this here town to the
fucking ground."

"Somebody said that?" he persisted.

"Somebody big said that could happen."

"Who?"

"Can't tell." She grinned at him, holding up her

index finger like a teacher speaking to a too-inquisitive child.

"Aw come on. You're with a friend."

"Naw. I can't." She belched heartily. "Torb told me not to. And I got to do what Torb says. Torb, he owns this here place. Exceptin' he don't own Sophie O'Govern." And she broke into peals of laughter.

Clint had what he wanted. The connection. He stood up, and just as he did so, Angie, the blonde from the Screaming Eagle, walked into the room. Clint remembered that she was friends with one of Sophie's girls.

"I'll be leavin' now, Sophie," she said, after grinning a big hello to Clint. "I got to get to work."

"You should leave the Eagle and come work for me," Sophie said, looking the girl up and down with an appraising eye.

"I'll walk you over," Clint said.

"Great!"

Over Sophie's protests that they stay and have another drink, they left the house. Clint was glad to get away, and not only because of Angie's company. He didn't like being around drunks, and he could see that Sophie was going to continue drinking until she fell flat. He'd gotten the information he needed anyway. Torb Mill's connection with the whiskey wagon, the booze and guns for the Shoshone. It wasn't something he could prove, not yet. But it fit. Torb—Ephraim Crosby's right-hand man. Torb—and Lilly Crosby. He was pretty damn sure now that it had been Torb he'd seen leaving the big brick house the other night.

For it was clear to him now that Mill was using the Indians as a threat. At the same time the threat of their rising up and killing whites could be a cover for something else. He didn't yet know what it covered, but he was sure it would reveal itself. The main thing was that he was satisfied that Runs-His-Horses wasn't planning any trouble, and that Mill was running a sandy on the town. He was doing it real easy-like. It was even casual. Clint had to admire the man's style.

Angie had said she was due to go to work right away.

"Couldn't I talk you into a little fun?" Clint said as they walked along Main Street.

"I'm late now. But . . ."

"But what?" he said, giving her arm a squeeze.

"But maybe you could help me get changed—uh—into my working clothes."

"I've always been a gentleman," he said gallantly. "I've never denied a lady's request. And I'm not going to start now, by golly!"

They both chuckled at that.

And shortly, in her room above the bar at the Screaming Eagle, they chuckled again as they undressed each other. Without hurrying, yet also without wasting a moment, their bodies came together on her bed, the springs clanging and whining in tune to their great pleasure. She gave him all she had, and he returned the delightful favor.

"I've got to go now," she said.

"Wouldn't you rather come?"

Her laughter tickled his ear. "You know the answer to that."

"You'll have to show me," he insisted.

She did.

NINE

At the precise moment that Clint Adams was putting on his trousers and saying good-bye to Angie, Torb Mill was lying naked and satiated beside Lilly Crosby—also naked and satiated—in her big double bed. It was a bed that her husband Ephraim had ordered from San Francisco, but not one in which he had pleasured himself with his young wife. Nor had he given his wife pleasure. This was an oversight he would rue, the consequence being his abrupt demise, though not by Lilly's hand.

At the moment Lilly was lying totally relaxed and happy beside her lover of the past three years. It was such a pleasant relief to be able to do it at home in her own bed, and without any worry over interruption. Like that terrible time they'd been doing it in Torb's office—on the floor—and guess who walked in! She still felt herself blushing at the memory of it. Well, he shouldn't have walked in. He should have knocked. It was not his house, though the greedy bastard thought he owned everything in town, including the people. He should

131

have knocked, and anyway, anyway, he asked for what
he got.

"Darling," she said suddenly, opening her eyes.

"Hmmmmm . . ."

"Darling, wouldn't it be fun to take a trip to Frisco.
I'd love to see the sights and do some shopping."

"It would be fun," he agreed, turning toward her,
and nestling his nose and mouth where her neck and
shoulder met. "But there's a tremendous amount of
work to do. Ephraim did leave things in a helluva
mess."

"But we could have such fun!"

"Maybe next month, when I've got things running
smoothly, and all the hullabaloo has blown over."

"Promise?"

"Promise." He sat up and looked at his watch.
"Damn. I've an appointment almost now. Well, in
twenty minutes."

"Will I see you later?" she asked, stretching.

"Wild horses . . ." he said, staring down at the pink
nipples that were still fresh from their lovemaking.

She reached down and felt his penis.

"Darling, I've got to go."

"I know you do. I'm not stopping you."

"You're giving a damn good imitation of stopping
me, young lady."

"I'll let him go," she said. "But just one kiss
before." And she bent down and took his rigid penis in
her lips, tickling its head with her darting tongue.

"I thought you had to go," she said in his ear as he
stroked his member into her.

"I thought so, too." He said into her hair.

• • •

"I know that. I heard that already," Torb Mill was saying as he leaned back in his big chair and surveyed Felix Porterhouse from behind his big desk.

Felix let it pass. He said, "The men were pretty rough with the woman Sophie. I mean, they beat her and I don't think that was very bright of them. They go too far and there'll be the law on us."

"The law is no problem, but the opinion of the good citizens of this fine town is important," Torb said.

"So what can we do about it?"

Torb grinned. "You could go on out to the Double Bar B and tell Bearing and Jesse and the boys that they are dumb."

"That's not funny, Torb."

"Oh, I've offended you. I am sorry."

But Felix had been practicing with himself, not to allow himself to get caught by Torb. He smiled. Carefully. "What about the Shoshones?" he asked, shifting ground. "The tribe doesn't seem to be cooperating with the whiskey and guns plan."

Torb leaned his elbows on his desk and supported his big chin with his laced fingers. "That's no problem, Felix." His baiting mood seemed to have passed. "First of all, they're not even a tribe, not anywhere near that size. They're a small band. Reduced through war and poverty. Sad but true."

"But what will happen, Torb? I'm not clear. Crosby was trying to get them removed; we all know that."

"Not all, Felix. Not anymore. You and I and that's it. Crosby knew it. And I have allowed you to know only in order for you to help me in, uh, certain areas.

For this I depend on your complete silence. You understand.''

Felix liked it when Torb was like this: confiding, serious, not trying to bait him, treating him in a good way.

"I understand, Torb.''

"We simply want to execute old Ephraim's plan, as per his wishes; and Mrs. Crosby's. That is, we want them Shoshones removed to another place. Those water rights nearby, which we will soon acquire, will be just what that tract of land needs. And with the new law allowing homesteading . . ." He spread his hands.

"But that can't be homestead land. It's Indian. It was ceded to them.''

"Of course." Torb was patient, kind. He had to be. He needed Felix, who was not very bright, but he was not only loyal, he was a good pupil as well. The one person on the council who would do exactly what he wanted without even a murmur. The others eventually did what he wanted, but always there had to be the arguing, cajoling, sometimes even threatening; and it all took time. As it had with Ephraim. Even the old man had sometimes had trouble with the council. Of course, he'd always won out in the end, and so had Torb; though on occasion having to defer to the old man. But not anymore!

"It's not that particular section there that's being opened for homesteading, but the land near it. Now, if we—I—control that piece—what is now Shoshone—we will control the whole valley.''

"Because of the water.''

"Go to the head of the class!" And Torb broke into

jolly laughter. We'll have a brandy on that," he said. And he reached for the bottle.

They drank and toasted their success. Felix felt he at last belonged, and he was glad to serve. What the rest of the council didn't know wouldn't hurt them, he told himself. He was learning such a lot from Torb. Hell, Torb was going to be even bigger than Ephraim.

A thought occurred to him. "So you've been figuring that the army or the law might move the Shoshone if it got around that they were drinking and had guns and so on."

"Precisely. Only their chief, Runs-His-Horses foiled that. So I've had to go to another plan. A much more dependable plan, let me swiftly add. Guaranteed to get us what we want."

"So there won't be any Indian uprising."

"Oh, but there will be! There will be, indeed!" Torb grinned hugely at the shocked surprise on Felix's face. "My man, there will be. People have been expecting an uprising and they will get one."

"You mean people will be shot—killed?"

"Not our people. Not the people in Sunshine Wells."

"But who?"

Torb Mill sat back in his chair. He leaned his elbows on the chair's arms and made an arch of his fingers, with one index finger touching his nose. He was smiling.

"Felix, you have learned something under my tutelage. But now you will learn a classic lesson. It is as follows: Never, never, never do what people expect. Always, always give the unexpected." He held up the palm of his hand in protest as Felix started to burst into speech.

"Enough! Watch and you will learn. Later we can talk. We can have one of our critiques. If you wish, of course. If you still wish to continue learning how to handle people and affairs."

"The hand of the master," Felix intoned, smiling as he lifted his glass of brandy to toast.

Torbert Mill inclined his head in acceptance of the accolade.

Clint had urged Harry Bones to wait, not to ride out to the Double Bar B with his warrants for the men who had beaten him.

"What the hell else can I do?" growled the marshal. "Except cold-cock the sons of bitches; which I'd like to. But I'm still a lawman. 'Course I could resign and go for 'em on my own." And he seemed really to be thinking of maybe doing just that.

"No, by God, I'm serving them!" And he picked up the papers that were lying on his desk, and which he'd been signing when Clint had walked in.

"Harry, it looks to me like I got here just in time. Look, you don't have a chance with all those guns. They'll bury you quick as a whistle, my lad. Are you looking to get yourself killed?"

Harry Bones seemed to hesitate. "I dunno," he said. "Maybe that's it. I dunno. All I know is I am going to bring them bastards in—hot or cold, I don't care which it is."

"It'll be you who's brought in," Clint said.

"You can't live forever." All the while Bones was talking he had been taking cartridges and shotgun shells from the gun cabinet and filling his pockets. Now he took down a cutdown twelve-gauge and loaded it.

Clint watched him almost in despair.

"What's this town going to do without a marshal?" he asked.

"It ain't got one now, my friend. Not so long as I let those buggers whip me. Least I'll be decent dead, not crawling alive, like too many I have seen."

And then Clint tried a wild shot. "That the way Cole Bonner would have handled it?"

The marshal of Sunshine Wells didn't take long to answer that one. "Cole Bonner is sweet dead, far as I ever heard," he said. And he looked at the Gunsmith plumb center.

"I do believe that is so," Clint said. "I only mention the name because it suddenly came to my memory. Fact is, I remember hearing of that gentleman way back, when I was younger, and I got the feeling of a good man."

"That newspaper feller, the one following you about; he come to see me."

"He thinks he's writing a book about me," Clint said.

"I got the notion he wants to write somethin' on Cole Bonner."

"Well, you know how those newspaper fellers are. They'll make up stuff. He did ask me a lot of questions; about me and the 'old days,' as he called them." Clint grinned then at the expression on Harry Bones's face. "I couldn't help him worth a damn. First thing, I am sick of this Gunsmith thing, and I would guess any old-timer from the old days would feel the same about himself. Leave things be, I told that greener, and try minding your own business.''

''Good enough,'' Harry said, working his Adam's apple some. ''Now we kin get back to it.'' And he checked the shotgun.

''You are still going?'' Clint asked.

''I am.''

''I'll make a deal with you.''

''Yeah? The law don't make deals. You oughta know that.''

''You need a deputy, right?''

Harry Bones put down the shotgun, laying it on top of the warrants on his desk. ''I'll be a shit-pisser if I ain't heard it all, right now.''

''I'll be your deputy. For as long as this action lasts, or we don't last. But you got to stick around, meaning no going out to the Double Bar B without your deputy.''

''Let's haul ass then.''

''Not so fast. We got to take a look at this thing. I mean, we have got to study it.''

''What you gettin' at?'' The marshal squinted at him, canting his head to one side.

''We have got to take first things first,'' Clint said. ''Take the most important thing before we look at anything else.''

''And which is. . . ?''

''Some of that arbuckle. I am in sore need of a good mug of coffee.''

''There is two things going here,'' Clint said, as he nursed his mug of coffee. ''First, the murder of Crosby along with the murder of Todd Gandy.''

"Providing you are figuring that last one to be a murder." The marshal's tone was sour. "I got to admit it more and more looks like it."

"Second, there is the riling up of the Shoshone."

"That is the important one for the town."

"I'd say they both are. Gandy is one man, but his getting killed, railroaded—lynched—you could put it, leaves a mark on this town that I would think any decent citizen would want to get rid of."

"I'll go with that. And I am planning to get hold of Bearing and his boys also on that charge. I want to go over those stories. Thing is, I'd been waiting for the Justice of the Peace to come by. He is due anytime now."

"You'll open it up then?" Clint asked. "While his widow is here?"

"I figger Mrs. Gandy's got the right to that. And I want to get to the bottom of the whole damn business and then be shut of it."

"And what about the Shoshone?" Clint asked. "How do you see that?"

"You got any idea who is sending them whiskey and guns?" Harry Bones asked. "I don't mean Bert; but who is back of him?"

"Best way to find that out would be to catch Bert, I'd say."

"That is what I am meaning," the marshal said. "I kicked Bert out and I ain't seen hide nor hair of him since, like I already told you. Now I don't know if you have heard anything about him being on Mill's payroll."

"No, I haven't. Is he?"

"I took a wild guess at it and said it to Torb, and he didn't say no. But I ain't sure one hundred percent."

"Could he be hanging out at the Double Bar B?" Clint asked.

"Likely." Harry Bones scratched into his big mustache. "I'd figgered to ride out and bring him in just before I got laid up; but I also got to thinking of leaving him. Give him rope for hanging himself."

There came a knock at the door of the office then, and Clint reached for his makings while the marshal shouted out that the door was not locked.

"I've brought you some hot soup," Kerry Joyner said as she walked in with a hamper. Then she saw Clint. "Gee, wish I'd known you were here. But maybe there's enough." She grinned at him and his heart raced. "Yes, I do think there's enough. And there's some fresh biscuits."

She simply took over the office with her laughter, her energy. There was no resisting her as she moved the papers on the desk, laid a cloth, and set out the soup plates and knives and spoons.

"As you see, I was sensible enough to bring extra crockery and spoons. That is called foresight."

"What you mean," said Clint, "is that you had planned to have dinner with the marshal. And I think you'd better do just that. Harry, we can talk later."

"Sit down, Mr. Adams." The words were said softly, but they carried the authority of a beautiful young girl who was absolutely sure of herself without being in the least bit conceited.

"Then you must join us," Clint said.

"I'm going to leave you."

"No!" The word came from both men in such unison that it was like one person speaking.

All three laughed then. And when Harry Bones wasn't looking, the girl let her laughing eyes wash over Clint Adams's face.

Clint stood up then and offered her his chair and walked over to an empty wooden crate to bring it over for himself to sit on.

"I'm off," Kerry said. "I will be back later for the plates. Oh, and there's some milk there for Steve," she added as she stepped lithely toward the door.

"Kerry, I'm gonna tell your dad you bin naughty," said Harry Bones, teasing.

"I'm always naughty," she said. "After all, I'm only just twenty-one!" And with a fantastic look at Clint, who thought he would have happily dissolved on the spot, she was gone.

Silence filled the marshal's office. Then Harry Bones spoke. "Looks like you made a good mark or two with the young lady."

There was nothing extra in his voice and Clint took it straight. "She's a great kid," he said, and was finally relieved to feel his blood slowing down to normal again.

They had their soup and biscuits in silence, and then took some coffee and lighted up their smokes.

"That gal would make some feller a good wife," Harry Bones said.

"I'll fade you on that one," Clint said. "But let's get back to business. I mean, I want to know more about Torb Mill. What have you got on him?"

Harry Bones didn't answer directly on that. He sat

easy in his chair, his eyes on the gray cat, who was washing himself in the pool of sunlight coming through the filthy window that faced onto an alley. It was just a big enough pool of light to encompass the whole of him except for the end of his tail. Suddenly, as though Steve himself had noticed the fact, he switched the end of his tail and wrapped it around his front legs as he yawned. The bath was apparently over.

"Damn animal's got more sense than most humans," Harry Bones observed. "You mind that, Adams?"

"Sure do. Cat takes care of himself and minds his own business."

"That he does." The marshal hawked, bringing up a lot of loose phlegm which he spat with accuracy into the coal bucket.

"A cat is a cat," Clint said. "But some men, I dunno."

"Some men I dunno what the hell they are," agreed Harry Bones. He scratched again into his thick mustache with his forefinger. "Now take a man like Torb Mill. He is a hard one to figure. On the other hand he's one-two-three, if you know what I'm drivin' at."

"You mean, once you've got him figured out then there's no worry over it."

"That's the size of what I am saying. You know a man like that's gonna slicker the drawers off a nun on Sunday morning, and then ask her to give him a helping hand."

Clint chuckled. "I understand he was Ephraim Crosby's boy."

"Huh! I'd say yes *and* no on that one."

"How do you mean that?"

"Torb worked for Crosby, sure. But he always had his own way, too. He worked for Crosby on the council, see. But then I always had the feeling that they had other business together."

"Sounds likely, from what I hear of those two men," Clint said. "But can you be more specific? What kind of business would they have together? Were they into something that you know about?"

"Only the real estate as far as I really know. But there could have been more. Exceptin' I don't know if Torb was really working for Ephraim or with him."

"Whether he was a partner, maybe?"

Harry Bones nodded.

"But now. Right now. Where does Crosby's death leave Mill?"

"He was number two on the council, after Ephraim; now he's number one. That's how they work it. Like Felix, he was number three, and now he's two."

"I got it. But Crosby's business, the real estate, would that go to his widow?"

The marshal nodded. "Sure would, and it has. She wanted it, and made no bones over it."

"Then that could mean Lilly Crosby and Torb Mill are partners—I mean, in the way, maybe, that Torb and Ephraim were. In the real estate, anyway."

"You hit it. Thing is, nobody knows who's got what. For the matter of that, nobody cares. What difference does it make?"

"None, unless you want to find a motive for getting rid of Ephraim Crosby."

"Jesus Christ." The words came from the marshal as a murmur.

"I am wondering if Crosby was back of the whiskey selling to the Shoshone," Clint said.

"You figger Mill is on that now?"

"I don't know. Only I saw Bert Smiles out there by that wagon. 'Course, the wagon was empty when I came on it, and I didn't hear any of them say anything that would incriminate themselves or anyone else. Anything I'd accuse them on they could just as easily deny it."

"You mean, they might have just happened on that wagon?"

"I know they didn't, but that's what they could claim and there's nothing to prove them lying."

"Shit," said Harry Bones. "Shit take it. We're right back at where we begun. Smells like a rat, looks like a rat, talks and thinks like a rat, does everything a rat does—exceptin' it's a donkey! Shit! Shit! Shit!"

"Nothing for a court of law, or the J. P.," Clint said.

"Sure ain't."

"Except we know Todd Gandy didn't kill Ephraim Crosby. And he was murdered because he didn't kill Crosby."

"What do you mean?"

"I mean if he had really killed him there wouldn't have been any need for that fake jailbreak and gunning him down so he couldn't testify and defend himself. Plus, all the rest: Crosby so far from home in the middle of the night, without his cane, no hat, which he always wore. And so on. Killed by a man supposed to be blind drunk. Hell, even an old man like Crosby couldn't have been attacked and killed by a man as drunk as Gandy was supposed to have been. Do I need to go on?''

"Nope." Harry Bones looked at Clint briefly, then his eyes swung to the ceiling. "Who do you figure killed him?''

"I don't know. But let's not forget that the real killer might have been someone who didn't use the knife himself.''

"You're saying the killing could have been ordered.''

Clint nodded. "Maybe. Maybe. On the other hand it might have been someone who was so all-fired mad at the old man that he just up and killed him on the spot.''

"And dragged his body to where it was found.''

"Maybe he had an accomplice, maybe not. But Gandy was handy. Slug him. A pistol barrel along the back of his neck. Pour some whiskey on him and lay him down next to the corpse.''

"With his hand on the knife.''

"That was what overdid it for me," Clint said. "Just that one detail spoiled it all for the killer, as far as I am concerned.''

"We've got no proof," Harry Bones said.

"Not unless we can get somebody to talk.''

"Who? Smiles? Heavy John Bearing and his boys? You can whistle for that.'' The marshal looked glumly at the Gunsmith.

"Know anything much about Lilly Crosby?" Clint asked suddenly.

"Only that she seems a nice enough person. Doesn't throw herself around much. Good-looking, like you can see.'' He paused and then added, "I'd say kind of on the young side for an old geezer like Crosby.''

"He was always in real estate, huh? Isn't that what you said?"

"Yeah. But there's nothing strange about that. Nothing secret. All I bin tryin' to get at is what he was doing on the side, if anything. On account of maybe he was doing nothing secret. Like you—hell—I'm just fishing around."

"Real estate," Clint repeated, almost to himself.

Harry Bones had been studying his thumb knuckle and now he looked up. "Whaddaya got?"

"Hunch. Lemme follow it before saying it." Clint was up on his feet. "Tell me something. Do you know if old Ephraim visited the cribs?"

"Could of. Hell, every man needs a chance to dip his wick now and again."

"He had that good-looking wife."

"It takes two to do it," the marshal observed sagely. "And maybe, maybe Ephraim had his likes and his dislikes."

"I am right with you on that one," Clint said as he started to the door. "Just want to look into something before I spoil it by talking it out too soon."

"Sounds interesting," the lawman said easily, with no expression on his face.

"One thing, though." The Gunsmith paused in the open door. "Ever hear of a Mrs. Wagner?"

"Should I?"

"She used to live here."

"Can't say I know the name." Harry Bones's brow tightened. "If I recollect it I'll let you know."

The marshal had risen and followed Clint halfway to the door. Now turning back to his desk he saw that the cat had taken his chair.

TEN

Clint kicked himself for not having thought of it earlier; and at the same time he knew it was nothing more than a straw, but it was there. And it had been there all along; ever since Jackie Gandy had mentioned Mrs. Wagner and that Todd Gandy had been doing something about her real estate. He couldn't hold out much hope, the whole thing as he saw it was so loosey-goosey he knew he was just looking for a miracle. But the name Wagner was stuck in his mind now. It was a chance; just a chance.

But first he wanted to make some inquiries before approaching the real estate office that sported the new sign on the white painted building on Main Street. First he wanted to be a little better acquainted with the ground.

The door was opened almost immediately following his brisk knock, and it was Sophie herself who stood there on the threshold, her flaming face and tinted hair looking like some strange fruit. A cigarette in a long holder almost stabbed him in the face as she stepped back and swept her arm toward the parlor in welcome. Her voice cracked like someone with severe laryngitis as she covered him with words.

"So good to see you, my dear friend. It's been such a long time . . . We missed you . . . We have a new girl . . . something delicious for your high-class tastes, I'm sure . . ."

The parlor was thick with the odor of perfume. There was no question where he was. If he'd been blindfolded he would have known what sort of house he had entered. It reeked of immoral pleasures.

Suddenly, as he seated himself in a chair, not on the sofa beside her where she had just patted a place for him, she stopped. Her features swept to an expression of alarm.

"Now, don't tell me you just came here to talk again," she said, and her voice rose, ending on a high note, almost as though she'd been suddenly goosed.

Clint grinned, like a schoolboy caught at the cookie box. "Sorry, young lady, but that's the way of it. I need your help."

"Might cost you something," Sophie countered severely.

"I haven't got any money.

"I'll take it in trade, my dear."

Clint, caught by the short hairs, swiftly plunged into the subject, heroically ignoring the business and social implications for the moment.

"I wanted to ask you if you knew anybody named Wagner. I mean some years back. I'd heard you'd been living in Sunshine Wells for a good while."

A strange interior sort of smile came into Sophie's

countenance at that point. "Boy, you got balls or somethin'; I mean, coming into a cathouse twice in a row and not sampling the merchandise but just askin' a bunch of damn fool questions. I ought to throw you out!"

"Sophie . . ." He tried his sheepish look, reserved for such occasions, and it worked. Something did. Actually, Sophie told him what it was that worked.

"It's my soft heart," she said, "that let's you stay. I swear I wouldn't for anyone else."

"How about Ephraim Crosby?"

"That old fuck!"

"Or Torb Mill?"

"That slimy bugger!" But she didn't let her irritation mount. "Who was it you asked about?"

"Wagner. A Mrs. Wagner. I don't know the first name."

"Mrs.!"

"I don't mean she was one of your girls. But someone in the town. Maybe she had a husband visiting you now and again."

He could tell that she was really trying, as she puckered her face, scratched under her left breast, and snorted. "Can't say I know the name. 'Least not in Sunshine here." And she sighed.

Clint was swift on the uptake. "You say not here, but where then?"

"There used to be a Wagner out on the North Fork. Had a wife, I think. Yeah . . . fact, I mind the time they come to town once on account of the Shoshone was actin' up, or threatening to. Them and another couple of families." She paused, searching her memory. "But I ain't seen either Wagner in a good spell. Might not be the one you're thinking of, anyways."

"Where did they live? It was just the man and woman, was it?"

"I do believe so. But it's a while back."

"And what about the Indians, the Shoshone?"

"Nothing. There was one of those alarms that come every once in a while; not so much as now, actually. See, there was like three families lived on the land where the Indians are living now, I mean, since the government or the army, anyways, moved them there. Before that they were nearby, but past Willow Creek. The Indians is what I'm sayin'. A pretty far piece from here."

"Are you saying that the families had to move because the army or Washington picked their place for Runs-His-Horses's Band?"

"I dunno why. Hell, I am not a history teacher or somethin'. Now, if you want to show some interest in *my* line of business, then let's get to it! Why don't you at least take a look at the girls? You don't have to have it with me. Maybe I'm too fancy for your taste, huh. Bet I could teach you a trick or two, mister."

"I bet you could, too, Sophie. But, uh, not now. And I want to thank you for your trouble."

"How about a drink?"

"Maybe later."

"Horseshit!"

"I'll be back," he said, standing up.

"Stripped for action, you better be!"

And they both broke into laughter at that.

With his hand on the front door handle he heard the step on the stair behind him and turned.

Abner Frolicher was coming down the stairs slowly. On his round face shone a saintly smile. He was obviously floating.

"Ah, Clinton," he said gently, his eyes mild with satiation. "A fine good day to you."

At Clint's side, the proprietress of the house snorted. "Holy shit!" But the tone was reverent with awe at the sight she and the Gunsmith were beholding.

"Looks like he's feeling no pain," Clint observed.

"I have been blessed," Abner said, speaking to the universe.

"What the hell you been doing upstairs all this time?" Clint asked. "Getting material for a book on girls?"

The observation very nearly brought Madam Sophie to her knees in mirth, as her shrieks of laughter rang through the house.

Upstairs a door slammed, while Abner, finally reaching the front door of the house, flushed crimson with embarrassment and joy.

Clint had visited the real estate office, but only a clerk was there at the moment, and so he'd left his name, saying he would come back later. "So you're figuring Gandy come here to look into Mrs. Wagner's property, and maybe shook somebody who got worried on it," Marshal Harry Bones said when Clint confronted him with his theory. The marshal had finally remembered the name Wagner; describing an old man on a piece of land right up where the Shoshone were now located. And he had remembered more as he talked about it with Clint Adams.

"That's what Jacqueline Gandy told me," Clint said, "but I didn't recollect it until just now. I mean, she didn't put any emphasis on why her husband had come to Sunshine Wells, only sort of mentioned it casually. The main thing, of course for her, was what happened to him."

"But you're thinking that whoever killed Ephraim found he could kill two birds with the one stone; by using Gandy as the murderer he also got rid of someone looking into the Wagner business, whatever that was."

"That's the size of it," Clint nodded in agreement.

"Can't prove a word of it," the marshal said.

"Yes, we can."

"How?"

"You been wanting to ride out to the Double Bar B, like a piss-ant with a hard on," Clint said with a grin. "Now's your chance."

"I bin aimin' to ride out to do some evening with those sons-of-bitches. It don't have nothin' to do with Gandy, or his cute-looking widow," he added, with a wicked smile at his companion. Then his face straightened. "I am serious, I am going right now. I ain't gonna wait. I waited for you to get some more stuff together. And maybe you got it, maybe you don't. But I am going."

They were in the marshal's office and now Harry Bones strode to the gun cabinet and began picking his weaponry.

"We'll be going together," Clint said, dropping his idea of visiting the real estate office again.

"Suite yourself," Bones said over his shoulder.

"I am your deputy, remember?"

"How'n hell could I've ever forgot?" He turned, let fly a streak of chewing tobacco and juice at the coal bucket, hitting the side and splattering spittle and tobacco all over the stove. Steve only just made it out of the way.

"We will need a plan," Clint said.

"I got it right here," Bones said, patting his holstered .44.

"We need a plan to get the whole bunch together," Clint said. "I mean, we've got to set something up."

The marshal suddenly stopped what he was doing and took a long look at his companion. "I am listening to you all along, Adams. I hear you. Thing is, we want to catch the sons of bitches in their own action. Right?"

"Exactly." Clint stood up, turned his chair around and sat down again, crossing his arms on the wooden back, his eyes on the other man. "We can trip them up. See, one way to do that is to go after them one by one. I mean, like, let's say Bert Smiles, the one who let Gandy out of your jail, and Bearing and any of his boys who shot Gandy, and Torb Mill."

"Well, I see you're smelling the connection between Mill and Heavy John."

"Thanks to a lady—I am saying a lady—named Sophie, I have turned my attention in that direction. But the point is things are so spread out. We'd best choose where we'll hit first."

"How about the Double Bar B?"

"How about going to the top?"

"Mill?"

Clint nodded. "I am studying it still. Trouble with that is . . . I mean, when you pick 'em off one by one, someone gets wind of it and skedaddles. Whereas if you get them all together somehow, that isn't so easy. You see what I'm saying."

"I did go to school for about a year, a year and a half," the marshal said sardonically.

Clint Adams grinned at the older man, appreciating the marshal's understated humor.

At that point there was a brisk knock at the door and Abner Frolicher walked in.

"Well, by cracky, here is the latest wrinkle in our problem," Harry Bones said. "What you got, Abner?"

Abner was out of breath, almost to the point of sweating. "I've just come from . . . from . . ." He threw his desperate brown eyes at the Gunsmith.

"Say it," Clint told him. "The whorehouse." He looked severely at Abner. "Right?"

Abner nodded, licking his lips and then he blurted out his message. "There's a whiskey wagon, more than one maybe, coming up from Charm Butte; heading for the Indian village; Runs-His-Horses bunch."

"Where'd you hear it?" Bones demanded. "Sophie's?"

"Just an hour ago." He looked at the Gunsmith. "I looked for you at the Drover's."

"Who told you?" Clint asked. "Was it Sophie or somebody else?"

"Sophie; and she told me to tell you."

"I guess we see who's marshal in this here town," said Harry Bones, sour as a lemon.

"Who's bringing the wagon?" Clint asked, standing up now.

"I believe somebody named Bearing is in on it. A funny name."

"Heavy John Bearing?" Harry Bones said.

"That's it. But also others. I had the idea it wasn't just one wagon."

"What about guns?" Harry Bones asked. "Did Sophie say anything about guns?"

Abner's face squeezed up tight like a rubber ball as he strained his memory. "Could have. The fact is, I am not sure. I wasn't listening too well at first; I mean till she mentioned yourself." He said this last to Clint.

"Jesus," said Harry Bones. "Man gets his snatch an' he don't give a shit if school keeps or it don't." He spat vigorously, getting the coal bucket plumb center, and wondered for an instant where the cat was. "We better haul ass," he said.

But Clint held up his hand. "It could be a trap," he said. "Let's study it a minute. I mean, how come Sophie got hold of this information?"

"I wasn't figuring on riding all over hell-to-breakfast lookin' for that whiskey train," Harry Bones said. "I was figurin' on heading for the Double Bar B."

"You think Sophie was setting something up?" Abner asked.

"I don't think so," Clint said. "I don't think she'd do that." He cocked his eye at Harry Bones.

"It ain't her style," Harry said.

"I remember now she did say something I thought funny. I mean, like, strange," Abner said, scratching his crotch briefly.

"What was that?" Harry Bones asked.

"She said, 'You can tell that Gunsmith I'd hate to miss out on our date.' "

"She said it like that?" Clint asked. "She called me the Gunsmith?"

"I think I'm quoting her exactly," Abner said. "But the thing was, the way she said it. I mean, like she was nailing some of those words right into me."

"Let's go then," Clint said.

"I want to come with you." Abner's voice was steadier than Clint Adams had yet heard it. There was no denying him.

"Get yer ass moving then," Bones said. "You know how to handle one of these?" And he handed him a gunbelt and holster in which was a bulky Colt .44.

"I—I never have. But I can learn."

The marshal of Sunshine Wells didn't waste any time. "You point this, and you pull this. Got it?"

"I got it."

"And never, *never* point it at anyone 'less you aim to kill."

Within the next five minutes the two men had mounted their horses and ridden down to the livery to pick a mount for Abner Frolicher. It was the same blue roan Abner had ridden before.

"Looks like he's glad to see you, Abner," Clint said. "Just remember to hold that off rein when you climb up on him. And keep his head up."

As they rode out of town Clint thought he saw Jackie Gandy on the porch of the Drover's Rest. It was just her back as she started through the front door of the hotel. He was just as glad she hadn't seen him. He only had time now for the grim business at hand.

He had no idea of what was going to happen, or even when, but he had stopped to leave the message at the Crosby Real Estate office that he was looking for Mrs. Wagner; and that should sure touch off something.

Clint Adams didn't believe in luck. He knew he was going to need the whole of himself; the very best of everything he had. And maybe more.

Heavy John Bearing was just what his name said he was. He was big, tough, heavy—all shoulders and hands. Someone once put it that he was a throwback to the mountain men of the early days. But Heavy John ran cattle. Always had.

Like all true cattlemen Heavy John knew the cow was a way of life; just as the buffalo had been for the Indian. The cow gave meat, soap, fat, and candlelight. Its hide became a man's clothing, often his shelter, too, the cover for his wagon bows, the rugs in his soddy or log house. Then, too, the cow provided rawhide for baskets, trunks, dough pans, chairs, and beds. You could hobble your horse with rawhide, and even shoe it. In the early days rawhide took the place of wood and iron. The lariat rope had been made of rawhide, and so were school blackboards, slates to write on, playing cards, tabletops.

For the red man, the buffalo had been sacred, while the cow, if not exactly sacred for the white man, was surely central to his life.

Heavy John Bearing was rawhide himself; some claimed his daddy must have been a bull; though never to his face. Heavy John had trail-herded north from Texas with his father, a man now part of the lively folklore of the West. He, along with Oliver Bearing, had fought the Comanche, the Sioux, and the Cheyenne. Heavy John was even tougher than Oliver, people said. And from the moment he'd ridden north to the Absorokas, he'd decided that this was the place for him to build his brand.

The redskin inhabitants there did not agree with him, nor— later—had the outlaws, a number of other cattlemen, and sometimes the law. None of this put a brake on Heavy John Bearing. He dealt with these enemies with the force that was his nature. And he had won.

But Heavy John found one thing he couldn't beat. And that was civilization. The West was changing. And Heavy John wasn't. He found his way of life challenged in a way he didn't always know how to deal with. He was a tough man, and he had always been honest; but he didn't always find the sodbusters, the homesteaders, and mostly the townspeople in the form of businessmen ready to meet him on his own ground. The lawyers were tricky, and the big cattle combines were even more so.

Then, Heavy John was getting older. At seventy he was still "tougher'n a cowpoke's piggin string," with which he'd truss a calf so he couldn't do anything but bawl his head off. And for a time he'd found his way around the Homestead law by staking a forty-and-found saddle-poke to some dollars and he'd prove up on a section of land and sell it back to you. Except—and it was a while back—Barney Wagner had decided to go back on his word and he'd kept his section of land.

Then the U.S. Government decided the public land adjoining the Double Bar B would make a good place

for a reservation—notably the Shoshone. Heavy John
had been ready to fight that all the way, with guns if
necessary; knowing he didn't have a whisper of a chance
to win. But then old Ephraim Crosby had appeared and
somehow pulled strings in places only he knew about,
and the Indians were moved elsewhere—save for a
small band at the Twin Creeks, right next to Barney
Wagner's six-hundred-forty-acre section.

Heavy John figured he could take that, so he took a
step back and was more or less content that he had
settled for something a whole lot less than the brunt of
the whole Shoshone nation at his back door—that is, on
his free range.

But he soon found that Ephraim knew more about the
situation than he did. It was Torbert Mill who informed
him finally that the "accident" that had happened to
Barney Wagner—getting thrown from his wagon by a
runaway team—hadn't been an accident. And the next
thing Heavy John knew he found himself connected up
to his neck, and maybe even higher, with Crosby and
Mill; and now, with simply Torb Mill.

It didn't take him long to discover the cause. It was
summed up in one simple word. Gold. Gold at the
Twin Creeks; right where Barney had homesteaded,
right where Runs-His-Horses was living with his band
of some sixty Shoshone.

The next thing that happened was the sudden and
unexpected demise of Ephraim Crosby, and his own
part in the episode of killing the accused murderer. It
seemed to Heavy John Bearing that he was getting in
deeper and deeper. But he told himself he still had his
ranch; he still was master of the Double Bar B.

And he told himself—not a few times, either—that by God nobody was going to take that away from him. They could mine all the damn gold they wanted anyplace they liked; he didn't give a damn; but he was going to run his brand. And no Injun, road agent, horse thief, lawman, or even that bitch down at the cathouse in town was going to make it different. He would bide his time, and he'd get shut of Torb Mill. Hell, there were times when he felt himself trussed like one of his round-up calves; and all he wanted to do was bust out. And he would, by God!

He was standing at the window of his ranch house looking out over the land he had known for so long and so well, when there came a knock at the door.

It was one of his hands who walked in, a stove-up old bronc-stomper who was only good enough for chores now like swamping out the bunkhouse and running messages.

"What can you tell me?" Heavy John said.

"He's on his way."

"Who brought it?" Heavy John turned to face the old broncobuster, who looked as though every bone in his body had caught it sometime or other. By contrast, the big body of his employer seemed to fill the room. The old man looked at the .44 at his boss's hip and he knew there was business afoot. For most of the time Heavy John Bearing didn't pack a gun. He didn't need to. But there weren't many men like that about.

"Bert Smiles spotted him down by Crazy Bear Crossing."

"He was alone?"

"Bert says yes."

"I hope that asshole Smiles didn't show himself," Heavy John said.

The old-timer nodded. His name was Swede O'Brien.

"He should be here anytime now," Heavy John said, turning back to the window. Then, "Where is Smiles now?"

"Out by the round corral. Him and Jesse are sackin' that little chestnut yearling. Looks to be a horse there, I'd say." And he followed this observation with a cackle.

"Tell Smiles and Jesse I want them."

When the old fellow was gone, Heavy John stood still in the middle of the room. Suddenly he discovered that he was looking down at the framed photograph of Ellie, the one that had been taken the year she died. That had been a while now, he was thinking as he picked it up from the small table by his easy chair and studied it. When he put it back he suddenly thought of Sophie O'Govern, and for just a split second he felt the force of the blow he landed on her that night in her parlor. Goddamn, he was thinking. Godammit to hell. He hoped he hadn't hurt her; even though the bitch had asked for it. Still . . .

He looked down at Ellie again, and then he walked to the window. He stood there, looking out at the long stretch that ran all the way down to Berry Creek.

When there came a knock at the door, he called "Come in." He knew without turning around that it was Jesse Ollinger and Bert Smiles. Christ, he could smell them!

"Got your message, boss," Jesse said to Heavy John's hard back.

"Rider," Heavy John said. He didn't turn from the window. "Down by the big rock."

He heard one of the men behind him reaching for the binoculars on his desk. Heavy John didn't take them.

"It'll be him," he said.

Jesse said, "I better rustle up some of the boys."

"I will handle this," Heavy John said.

"Sonofabitch is quicker'n smoke," Bert Smile said. "We can cover him, boss. Fact we had men flanking him all the way in."

"That's what I know, you dumb shit—seein' as how I ordered it."

A silence fell now as the two men behind Heavy John waited.

"You get out to the men and tell them to watch what I sign. I don't want anyone trying to draw on that fast sonofabitch, but set up for crossfire the way I showed you. But you wait for my signal. Tell them that! Now get out of here!"

He had not taken his eyes from the rider, still standing with his back to them as he gave the order, and they closed the door.

Heavy John continued to stand there as the lone rider disappeared behind a stand of cottonwoods. He was going to follow the road around the side of the ranch, and the man at the window knew exactly the place where he would reappear.

Now, even though the rider was out of sight, Heavy John Bearing continued to stay at the window, waiting for the Gunsmith to ride closer.

Yet strangely, he found he was not thinking about his dangerous visitor. He found that he was thinking about

Ellie. He wondered why at this particular moment she should come to him like this.

And he discovered, too, to his astonishment that the image of Sophie O'Govern had invaded his mind. He couldn't understand that, and he didn't even try. Only why had he thought of his wife, and why especially had he thought of that old bag who ran the town cathouse?

He suddenly shook himself. Hell, this was no time for thoughts. Things were coming to a place between hard and hard. And he needed to be clear.

He unbuckled his gunbelt then and tossed the rig onto the chair next to Ellie's photograph. But he wasn't thinking of Ellie now. Not at all. He was thinking only of how he was going to get rid of that sonofabitch on that big black horse who was faster than light and could shoot the eyelashes off a grizzly without that beast knowing enough to even blink.

ELEVEN

"Dammit! Damn!" Torb Mill stood in the office of Crosby Real Estate and stared at Lilly, who was seated at Ephraim's old desk. "Did anyone else hear that Adams was looking for Edith Wagner, other than Katey?"

"Not as far as I know. And I told her to keep it absolutely quiet." A sigh ran through Lilly Crosby's body. "Torb, he's up to something, that man. He can upset everything."

"You're not telling me anything I don't already know," he snapped. "Dammit! He must have heard about Wagner from Gandy's widow."

"But you've gotten her signature for a sale, after all, Torb."

"It's not a legal, binding document. The thing is for the old lady to keep her mouth shut. I'd better get right out there, just to see if Adams or anyone has been snooping around the place. Then, you write a letter to the old lady and send it to her. Tell her about Ephraim; tell her that the property's being taken care of, and not to listen to anyone other than me and yourself. She's living with her daughter.''

"Where? Back in the town Gandy came from, isn't it?''

"That's right.''

He calmed down somewhat. "Hell, there isn't anything Adams can find out there that would make him suspicious.''

"There aren't any gold filings left about, are there?'' she asked.

"I had some men clean the whole area. And I checked it myself only a couple of weeks ago.''

"Maybe Adams is just trying to flush something,'' she said.

"Probably. Yes, probably. I wouldn't be surprised. Because he doesn't have anything real. Anyway, it was a good long while ago that Wagner lived out there. Most people around here don't even know the place exists.''

Mill had started to pace the floor as he spoke his thoughts aloud to Lilly, and now he stopped, his face composed in thought.

"I wonder,'' he said.

"What? What do you wonder? Torb, do sit down, you're making me nervous. And I don't think there's any real reason for either of us to be nervous about a thing.''

He wasn't listening to her; he was wrapped in thought. He turned then, as she pushed back from the desk, and looked at her quietly, his finger raised to make a point. "Look, there's nothing anyone could find out at the old Wagner place. And there is nothing even here in this office. Everything we have on that situation is clean and aboveboard.''

''So then, what are we worried about? I ask you? I mean . . .'' And she shrugged and looked around the room as though searching an answer.

''Adams is no fool.''

''I'll take your word for that.''

''In fact, he's smart as a whip. Now then, how would a smart whip think? At this stage of the game when he still hasn't a strong hand, he'd have to bluff. Am I right?''

She leaned forward now, watching him intently, a slow smile coming to her face.

''He'd try to pull a quick one on us.''

''I am right with you, Torb. You're saying that the Wagner message is a decoy of some kind.''

''A decoy, a feint; an effort on Adams's part to flush something.''

''That certainly makes sense.''

''Exactly!'' He raised his forefinger high in positive assertion. ''And I am a step ahead of him.''

''We?''

He grinned at her. ''Of course, my dear. Habit. Forgive me. We are ahead of him. We would think one thing, look for him in one place, but he would be just at another place which we might well have left unattended.''

''Then the question is, what did we leave unattended.''

''Or, better, where is our weak spot?''

''Not on the council.''

He nodded. ''Not on the council.''

''Then?'' She had risen to her feet and was watching him, an expression of delight on her beautiful face.

"Bearing. The Double Bar B. Ten will get you twenty, my dear, that Adams, and maybe Bones, too, has ridden out to the Double Bar B."

"Will John be expecting him?" she asked.

"He had better be. I have told him to be ready—just in case. And he has Bert Smiles out at Crazy Bear Crossing as lookout. I sent him," he added.

"What do we do then, sit and wait?"

There was a grim smile on his face as he looked at her. "I suggest that you do that, my dear. I will be riding swiftly to the Double Bar B."

She came toward him swiftly. "But Torb, can't John Bearing handle it? I mean, stay here. We can be together."

"Darling, it's a tricky situation, and I'm the only one who can handle it. Bearing's a good man, but he needs somebody who is better."

"You'll be careful."

"I will." He was already opening a drawer in another desk across the room, and removing a handgun and extra cartridges. "This is the right moment to settle everything."

She had started to come closer to him to embrace him, but there came a brisk knocking at the door, and she stopped in front of him, and then quickly moved away.

"Come in," Torb called.

It was Felix Porterhouse who entered.

"You're just the one I want to see," Torb said. "We're going in my gig. Come on." A shaft of irritation ran through him as he saw the dumb surprise on Felix's face, but he ignored it, and smiled at Lilly for the intruder's benefit. "I'll see you when I get back," he said, in the tone of voice he always used for Ephraim Crosby's wife.

He had the scattergun under the yellow slicker on his pommel. Riding up from Crow Creek, past the big butte and out in full view of the Double Bar B he knew he could be picked off as easy as swatting a drowsing deer fly, but he knew that it was the time for boldness, that any small move would be taken as weakness. There was nothing else he could do anyway, if he was going to help Jackie Gandy. Hell, a man had to play the cards as he got them.

Now he could feel the sun hot on his back as it dipped closer to the western horizon, and when he shifted in his saddle he felt it on the back of his neck.

He had spent more than an hour with Harry Bones and Abner going over their plan. Harry had drawn a map in the dirt by the side of the trail, using a stalk of sage as a scribing tool. And he reckoned that by now the two men would be in position with the Sharps buffalo gun and the Winchester .44-.40, both from the marshal's gun cabinet. He was counting on Harry's savvy to catch anyone trying to cut their trail.

As for himself, he would be in the middle of it. The target. But he had also quizzed Harry Bones on Heavy John Bearing, going over details so that he felt he really knew the man—knew him maybe even better than if he'd actually met him. And so for one thing, he would bear in mind Heavy John's way as a cattleman of the old school. He knew the code; had lived it. It was vanishing from the country pretty quickly, but John

Bearing was still a man of the old code. Tough, rough, even brutal, but in a certain way, clean. Heavy John Bearing—Clint felt he could safely say this—was no bushwhacker; he wouldn't shoot a man in the back. By the same token, Torb Mill wouldn't shoot a man in the front. Yet each had the drive of the fanatic. Each one wanted, demanded his due—whatever that might be—from life. And took it. Torb with the cloak; Heavy John with his fist.

So it was a time for boldness.

Now his eye caught a rider off to his right just slipping down a draw, while to his left another outrider was cantering along a low cutbank.

Clint felt more at ease when he reached a stand of box elders and dropped from sight of the ranch houses. Yet he knew he was still accompanied. He spoke softly, but urgently to Duke now and the big black lifted his gait as he rode up a shallow incline and came all at once right onto the Double Bar B's bunkhouse.

The Gunsmith did not hesitate as he saw a half dozen men come out of the bunkhouse and stand there facing him, their hands close to their weaponed hips.

Then someone saw the slicker that was lying across the pommel of the Gunsmith's stock saddle.

"Look out, boys, he'll have somethin' under that slicker, for sure."

"We can still take him," someone else said. "There is six of us. Hey, Gunsmitty boy, what you want?"

"I am here to see John Bearing," Clint said in a flat tone. And when he heard the men moving up behind him he lifted his voice. "You men behind me, come out here in front. You make me nervous and I wouldn't want this cutdown Greener to go off by accident.''

He had slipped his hands down under the slicker, and now he moved it a little in emphasis of what he was saying.

''And you, you who called me Gunsmitty, go get Mr. Bearing.''

The young tough had paled slightly, but now he sneered in an effort to recapture his place; and said nothing.

''I am saying right now, sonny.''

''There is six of us.''

''So who will the three, four, five be who catch the first load of blue whistlers? You one of them, sonny?''

The men from behind him had moved around to the front where Clint could see them.

''That is better,'' he said. ''Don't spread! Stay close together. You hear me? A man can't miss with a goose gun like this.''

Suddenly a man in the back spoke up. ''Let's take a look at it! I am wonderin' if you got anythin' under that slicker.''

''There is a way you could find out, mister,'' Clint said.

At that moment the door of the ranch house opened and heads turned. Big John Bearing stepped out.

''I am unarmed, Adams,'' he said.

''I am not. So get these men away. I don't like crowds. And we can talk. But first, I want also a man named Jesse, and those other two who shot Todd Gandy; plus I want Bert Smiles.''

''On what authority do you think you're going to pull

that shit, Adams?'' Heavy John Bearing stood stolid as
a bull buffalo right in front of Clint and Duke.

In a trice, the Gunsmith had dismounted and stood in
front of his host, the shotgun in his left hand, with his
finger on the trigger.

Suddenly he caught a movement out of the side of his
eye, as one of the twelve swept his hand toward his
holstered six-gun. In the same instant a shot rang out
and the man screamed in pain, reeling back, clutching
at his shoulder. ''Forgot to tell you I got the outfit
covered with Winchesters and Sharps. That was a Sharps,
and the man handling it isn't going to hit anybody in
the shoulder next time.''

''You're bluffing, Adams. Cut the shit!'' snapped
Heavy John.

''Want to see if I'm bluffing?'' And then, sizing his
man right to the quick he said, ''Hell, I am not bluffing
any more than you were when you beat up on that old
lady Sophie O'Govern, you hero!''

He watched the color drain from the rancher's face.
Then he called out, ''All you men, unbuckle. I mean
fast!''

''Adams, I've got outriders . . .''

''No, you haven't,'' Clint said. ''See, I know you,
your kind. You fall for the razzle dazzle, a man riding
in here alone with all your guns ready to wipe him out.
That impressed you, and you were curious. And you'd
seen what I did to that little sonofabitch who tried to
draw on me in the Screaming Eagle. So all your attention was right here, right in front of your house. And all
my men are out there, covering you. Did you really

think I'd be so dumb as to ride in here all alone without being covered?''

He took a step toward Big John Bearing. ''Did you?'' And in that split second he saw something flick in the big rancher's eyes.

Later, nobody had the same story on what exactly happened. Except for one thing: one of the men, unbuckling his gun by the water trough had dropped his belt, but had come up with iron in his fist. He never got his weapon to the horizontal before the Gunsmith had drawn and shot him right through the heart.

Following that brief moment, nobody was interested in arguing the point.

''What is it you want?'' Heavy John Bearing asked.

''I want you, Jesse Ollinger, and Dink Wilson, and Bert there. You're under arrest. You'll ride back with me to town and you'll stand trial for the shooting of Todd Gandy; not to mention that all of you will undergo a good bit of questioning from Marshal Harry Bones and likely some of the town council, and for sure the J.P.''

''You'll never get away with it, Adams,'' Heavy John said. ''I've got a dozen men at Pitchfork Line Camp. They'll be riding. I was expecting trouble.''

''I am getting away with it, Bearing. It is you and your boys who aren't getting away with it. You'll stand fair trial for the shooting of Todd Gandy. Meanwhile, you'll come with me.''

''I still don't accept your authority, except for that what you got in your hand,'' Heavy John said.

''I am acting deputy marshal for Sunshine Wells.''

"Where is the marshal? Where is Harry Bones?" Bearing demanded.

"I would guess he'd have that Sharps reloaded by now. You want him to fire it again on the buffaloes?"

Nobody said anything to that.

"Now let's get going."

Clint ordered one of the men to collect all the guns while his prisoners got ready to ride into town with him.

"We'll make it to town after dark," he said when they were ready to ride out. "Don't be dumb enough to think you can try anything."

They weren't. It wasn't late, though the sun was down when they reached Sunshine Wells.

Harry Bones and Abner Frolicher showed up within the next hour and the prisoners were locked in. Abner was beaming.

"Any sign of Mill?" Bones asked after Clint had told him of the action at the Double Bar B.

"Nary a one," Clint said. "I would have thought he'd come out or something or other, but maybe he saw how we had everything pinned down. By the way, Harry, that was pretty slick shooting with the Sharps."

For a moment the Gunsmith thought the marshal of Sunshine Wells was going to uncork, and he suddenly caught the crimson flush all over Abner's tiny face and the wild look in his eyes.

"What's the matter with you men?"

When Harry Bones caught his breath, he was able to make some sense of it. "Reckon we ought to just leave it at that, Clint. I mean, like it was real fancy shooting,

catching that feller right in the moment like that. I
mean, when it was real necessary like you just explained.''

''That is what I am saying,'' Clint insisted, glaring at
his two companions as though there was something the
matter with them.

''Only thing is,'' Harry said, ''it wasn't me did the
shootin'.''

Clint Adams felt his jaw drop. His eyes moved to the
totally stricken Abner Frolicher, who was still flushing
a furious scarlet and nearly stuttering with excitement.

''You . . . !''

Abner was nodding his head, unable to speak.

''Holy smokes, Abner.'' He looked at Harry Bones.
''And you by golly were telling him how to handle a
gun! Aren't you ashamed of yourself.''

''Can I, Abner?'' The marshal's tone was pleading.

Abner could only gasp as he nodded his little head
again. Harry Bones had a look in his eye that Clint had
never seen before.

''See, Adams, you heard me tell him how to handle
that .44, but I never told him the best way to handle a
Sharps buffalo gun is to slip in some wet horseshit
when somebody asks you to hand it to them!''

They had driven out in the gig but had been late in
reaching the Double Bar B. Coming in over the lip of a
low draw they had spotted the small cavalcade leaving
the ranch.

''You see what I mean about Bearing not being very
smart,'' Torb said furiously. ''Now we've had a fruit-
less trip out here. We'll head right back and see what
we can do.''

They returned to Sunshine Wells in near silence, but Felix could feel Torb Mill's mood dropping dangerously. It was uncomfortable being with the man when he was like this; in one of his black moods. Felix had encountered this event seldom—maybe three times in the whole of his relationship with Torbert Mill, but he told himself it was three times too many.

By the time they reached Sunshine Wells, Felix couldn't wait to get away. Quickly he said his good-bye and took the rig down to the livery and turned it over to the hostler.

He had just said good-night to the old man when a boy came running into the livery with a message for him. It was a summons from Torb.

Somehow, Felix took his time getting to Torb's house. For once in his life he didn't feel that great need to be around the man; the fear when he was summoned. Was it because of how the Gunsmith had aced them? he wondered.

He found Mill in a fury. "Where the hell were you, for Christ's sake—down at the cathouse? I sent that kid for you a half hour ago!"

And again Felix found himself astonished at his own new attitude in the face of Torb's anger. It was indeed as though Clint Adams had defeated Torb, beaten him in some kind of invisible combat of wills. For the first time Felix began to feel different toward the man he had feared for so long; and—more important—to acknowledge it. And again he asked himself how much of it was due to Clint Adams. Or was it himself changing, getting older? He was really seeing Torbert Mill in a

completely new way. And his own next words under-
lined it for him.

"What can I do for you, Torb?" he asked, and
watched it hit the other man.

"You mean, don't you, what can *I* do for *you*,
Porterhouse!"

Felix said nothing, as he felt something of the old
way grab him inside. Yet it wasn't so bad. Not really so
bad! Formerly when that grabbing had occurred it had
all but cut off his breath, terrified him. But now—now
he could actually handle it.

"I don't like the idea of John Bearing spending the
night in jail," Torb said.

"I know. I don't either."

"Somebody might get scared or something and talk.
You know how people are."

"I can't see John Bearing talking out of line," Felix
said.

"You can never tell with someone like that," Torb
countered. "He's an old-timer. Some of those old boys
have different rules than the newcomers in this country."

"You're saying he's honest," Felix said sardonically, and was again astonished at his tone.

"I'm saying you cannot tell what such a man will do
under certain circumstances."

"What do you want to do then?" Felix asked.

Torb had been sitting down, and now he stood and
took a turn up and down the room. "I think we have to
get those men out of jail."

"You mean, like before?"

"Before? With Gandy, eh?"

"I'm asking, Torb."

"If certain things are said we could all be in trouble,"

"I know, Torb."

"Big trouble, Felix.

Suddenly Felix heard himself saying, "But I had nothing to do with any of that, Torb."

Torb Mill had started another turn around the room, but stopped and looked at Felix Porterhouse.

"I will overlook that remark, Felix."

Felix felt his insides dropping, and he thought he was going to be sick.

The long silence that followed was interrupted by a loud knocking at the door.

"So late at night?" Torb moved quickly to his desk and opened a drawer. For a moment he stood behind the desk looking at the number-two man on the council. The knocking came again, and it seemed louder.

"Felix, open the door. I believe we know who it is."

When Clint Adams and Harry Bones walked into the room, Torb was still standing behind his desk.

"Close the door, Felix. Gentlemen, what can I do for you at this, I must say, rather late hour of the night."

"We've got some questions for you, Torb," said Harry Bones.

"At this hour? Can't you wait until morning?"

"I think we won't be long," the marshal said. "We— Clint Adams—my deputy—and myself have just heard the confessions of Bert Smiles, Jesse Ollinger, and Dink Wilson."

A strange smile came into Torb Mill's face, while

Felix watched him in fascination. "Confessions? About what?"

"Confessions to the shooting and killing of Todd Gandy."

"You mean the man who murdered Crosby and was caught escaping jail."

"The man who was set up by Bert Smiles, who let him escape. The boys have confessed, Torb. There's no need for all of this now."

"The boys, you say? And what about Heavy John? I heard you brought him in, too."

"Heavy John says he didn't actually shoot Gandy, though he was present; and his men back him on that. But he will be questioned by the J.P. And I'm releasing him. John . . ." And he threw a glance at Clint, who was standing beside him, "John wants to clear things up. He's talking about cleaning the record. So we'll see."

Torb had stepped from behind his desk now and stood closer to his two visitors, while Felix had moved a little to one side.

"Well, congratulations, gentlemen," Torb said. "And now while I'm glad to hear that things are under control, and justice has triumphed, I must ask you to excuse me. It is . . . late." And he smiled.

To Felix, who was watching him closely, the smile seemed forced.

"That leaves the murder of Ephraim Crosby," Harry Bones said. "It's clear to anyone now that Gandy was innocent, and that somebody pinned the killing on him."

"Oh, yes, I see." Mill coughed quietly into his fist and turned back to his desk. Standing again behind it,

he faced Clint Adams and the marshal. ''I wish you
good luck. I'm afraid I can't be of much help there. In
fact, I'm sorry that the whole grisly episode has to be
reopened; but I guess there's nothing for it. We must
find the true killer then.''

''We have found him,'' Harry Bones said.

Felix felt his head swim, and suddenly all his new-
found freedom had vanished. He looked at Torb, wanting more than anything else to know what to do, how to
be. Completely forgotten now was his sudden taste of
being his own man. There was no question about it, he
would have done anything simply to shine in the eyes
of Torb Mill.

Fascinated, unable to move or speak, Felix watched
as Torb stepped farther behind his desk. He knew, he
would have bet his life on it, that Torb had something
up his sleeve, that he would turn the situation in his
favor the moment he wished to do so.

He was totally unprepared for what happened then.

Torb was speaking. ''Well, Felix, I am sorry. You
have been a most faithful, loyal, and dependable man.''
Torb was looking right at him, and now turned his eyes
to Harry Bones and Clint Adams. ''I am sorry to lose
Felix, gentlemen. And I am afraid I must accept my
share in not telling you sooner what I had only recently
begun to suspect. But I only began to put things together during the last couple of days. Now I see the
grim truth. But I didn't want to come and tell you
simply my suspicions; I had hoped, I prayed that I was
wrong. And I have no proof, Harry. I leave that up to
you.''

Felix stared in stunned agony as the words came smoothly from Torb Mill's mouth.

Torb was speaking again. "Felix, my friend, I will do all that I can to help you. I want you, and everyone present, to know that I am not deserting you in your hour of need."

It was then that Felix broke. All he could utter was an astounding, inarticulate scream of fury as he charged across the room toward Torb.

The big desk was in his way and he threw himself on it to get at Torb, thus blocking the view for Clint and Harry Bones.

In that instant Torb reached into the half-open desk drawer and came up with a handgun.

His first bullet never left its chamber. The Gunsmith had already killed him with a shot between the eyes.

It was over.

It was a shaken, but basically a very different Felix Porterhouse who took over the duties of number-one man in the Sunshine Wells Council. Quietly he explained to the members what had happened. Piecing it all together wasn't hard, he told them, especially with the man known as the Gunsmith leading it.

Todd Gandy's name was cleared, and Torb Mill was revealed as the murderer of Ephraim Crosby. Lilly Crosby had abruptly left town, but circulars were out in the necessary places. It was supposed that she could well have been an accomplice.

The dealings initiated by Crosby and carried further by Torb Mill were also revealed; the dealings regarding the discovery of gold at the Twin Creeks and the effort to get the Indians moved on the excuse that they were drinking and making trouble were also aired. Chief Runs-His-Horses had received the delegate from the town council with his usual equanimity. When informed by the new number-two man, Bob Belden, that his people were innocent of whiskey and gun-running, the chief had said—through his interpreter—that he also knew his people were innocent.

On hearing of Runs-His-Horses' reply, the Gunsmith smiled. From the way the conversation had been reported by Bob Belden to the council and relayed by Felix to Clint, he was pretty sure the chief's quality of humor had been entirely lost on the council members. Clint didn't mind. For him such a moment was special, because a man had to be in a certain way to give it, and also to receive it. Such people were few and far between. Runs-His-Horses was one, and the man who had been Cole Bonner, the famous highwayman and who was now Harry Bones, marshal of Sunshine Wells, was another.

The best of the whole affair for Clint was when he broke the news to, first, Sophie O'Govern, and then to Jackie Gandy. He had saved Jackie for the second news-telling, the moment with Sophie being necessarily short.

"I want to order a gravestone for Todd," Jacqueline told him when she had dried her eyes.

"Of course," he said.

"I don't know how to thank you, Clint. Really, you have been . . . I don't know how to thank you."

"Why don't we have dinner and I'll think up a way," he said, smiling brightly at her.

"Yes. Yes, and maybe I'll think up something," she said.

Later, which shortly became much later, they found a way together.

"How wonderful that we found the same way to thank you," she said as he rolled off her.

"Great minds seem to find each other, don't they," he said. "I've often heard that."

"And great bodies," she said grinning up at him as he raised up on his elbow and looked into her face.

"You have a superb body," he said.

"And you—you have a superb . . . everything," she whispered. "Thank you, thank you, Clint."

"You've already thanked me," he said, "And don't forget I had a lot of help."

'I'm thanking you for something else, my friend. I'm thanking you for making me happy again. For helping me to live again."

"I accept your thanks. And so does he," he added as he stroked his erection between her legs.

Meanwhile, in another part of town Abner Frolicher was holding court. This was at that favorite watering place for the residents, travelers, cow waddies from surrounding ranches, and also gamblers, and those whom the fancier writers of the eastern magazines referred to as "Cyprians".

Abner was right in the middle of one of his more lurid stories, embellished boldly in its numerous retellings, when he saw the Gunsmith enter the establishment. And he was brought up short.

"Like to see you a minute, Abner," Clint said, and

as the small crowd dispersed he and his would-be biographer found a table at the back of the room where they could speak in confidence.

"Abner, I have been hearing some of your stories around town, especially the one where you claim you're going to write a book about yours truly."

"I have been telling people—who wanted to know, Clint—about my adventures, and also my plans as an author."

"There's not going to be a book on me, Abner," Clint said, leaning close to him. And as Abner started to protest, he added, "Nor on Cole Bonner."

"But, Clint . . ." Abner's thin face seemed to fall all the way to his small chest.

"I mean it, Abner."

"All right. If you say so."

"I want to be sure, Abner."

"I promise not to write anything about you or about Harry."

"Can you keep your promise, is the question," Clint said.

"Oh, I can. I will keep my promise!"

Clint leaned forward, lowering his voice even more. "Abner, just to make sure. I want you to remember that there are two people in the West who know exactly how that Double Bar B cowboy was shot. And it is not the way you've been telling it, Mister Hero."

Abner Frolicher blushed furiously.

"You understand what I am saying, Abner?"

"I do. I do, Clint. I understand! I promise!"

"It would be terrible if a famous author's readers

ever heard such a story. And of course, neither Harry nor myself would ever spread it. Unless—''

"Clint, my lips are sealed!"

The sun was throwing its last rays across the town when Clint came out of the Screaming Eagle, and started down Main Street.

He was thinking how he had better get to his gunsmithing, remembering how Doc Joyner had said he had a couple of firearms that needed work.

He was also thinking of saying hello to Kerry Joyner, who had informed him with such emphasis that she was all of twenty-one. He thought that delightful. And then he remembered that Jackie Gandy would be heading back East in a day or two, and so there wasn't going to be much time left for being thanked.

As he walked quietly down the street now with the long, slanting sunlight washing over him and through him, he chuckled. Jackie Gandy—Kerry Joyner.

He was thinking how people so often complained about not being able to make up their mind about something; but for him now he could only feel delighted at the marvelous indecision that he was facing.

Watch for

WINNER TAKE ALL

eighty-fifth novel in the exciting
GUNSMITH series

coming in January!

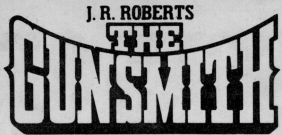

J. R. ROBERTS
THE GUNSMITH
SERIES

SONS OF TEXAS

Book one in the exciting new saga
of America's Lone Star state!

TOM EARLY

Texas, 1816. A golden land of
opportunity for anyone who dared
to stake a claim in its destiny...and
its dangers...

Filled with action, adventure,
drama and romance, *Sons of Texas*
is the magnificent epic story of
America in the making...the
people, places, and passions that
made our country great.

Look for each new book in the series!